Murder in Cold Springs

Peter D. Cameron

Contents

Dedication

To my Family; my wife, son, and daughter in law. They are the rock upon which I stand. This is for you, for all your encouragement and support. Without it, this would never have happened.

Acknowledgment

To Lyn O'Brian, the Town Clerk of Otis, the Otis Preservation Trust and the Otis Historical Commission especially Tom Ragusa. Their belief in the history of their town led me to write that history and discover this story.

To the English Department of Cheshire High School in Cheshire Ct. for all their help, and especially Maureen Reed for her constant encouragement.

About the Author

Peter grew up at the family-owned vacation home in Otis, Massachusetts, thus his interest in the area. He is a retired Police Lieutenant of the Wallingford, Connecticut Police Department. He graduated at the age of 48 from Central Connecticut State University with a degree in history. His first book Norton Cemetery: May we never forget, published in 2013, is a history of Otis, Massachusetts. It was during his research for the first book that he discovered this story. He and his wife reside in Wallingford, Connecticut, and still own the vacation home in Otis.

Preface

This is the story of a triple homicide that occurred in the Cold Springs section of Otis, Massachusetts, in September 1862. Newspaper records, court transcripts and town records have allowed me to tell the story with remarkable accuracy. It follows, in detail, the investigation, prosecution, and punishment of those responsible.

Police techniques in 1862 were certainly not as advanced as they are in the 21st century. Fingerprints and DNA evidence were unheard of. Recognizing this, I have used the available resources to tell this story accurately, relying first upon information available and absent the standard investigative techniques common in the 19th century.

I have painstakingly attempted to remain faithful to the details of the case. Many of the names, places, dates, and occurrences are accurate, drawn from census records, old maps, and Berkshire Eagle newspaper archives. Despite this research, there were areas, such as individual personalities and some identities, where information and details were simply non-existent. I was forced to invent information to fill those areas to tell the complete story. That being said, I have tried to remain faithful to the story, the history and society of the time and region, and my twenty-five years of law enforcement knowledge. This is a work of historical fiction, but it accurately reflects this incident as it took place in 1862 and 1863.

I have included the following two maps to give the reader the location where this took place, identifying important locations as referenced in the book.

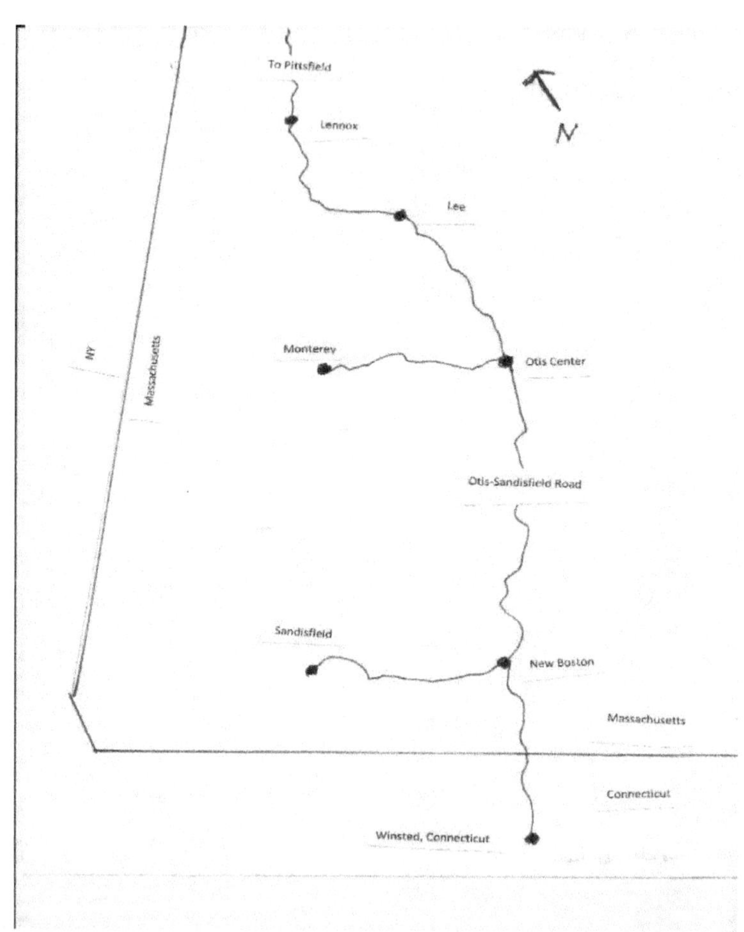

To Pittsfield
Lennox
Lee
Monterey
Otis Center
NY
Massachusetts
Otis-Sandisfield Road
Sandisfield
New Boston
Massachusetts
Connecticut
Winsted, Connecticut
N

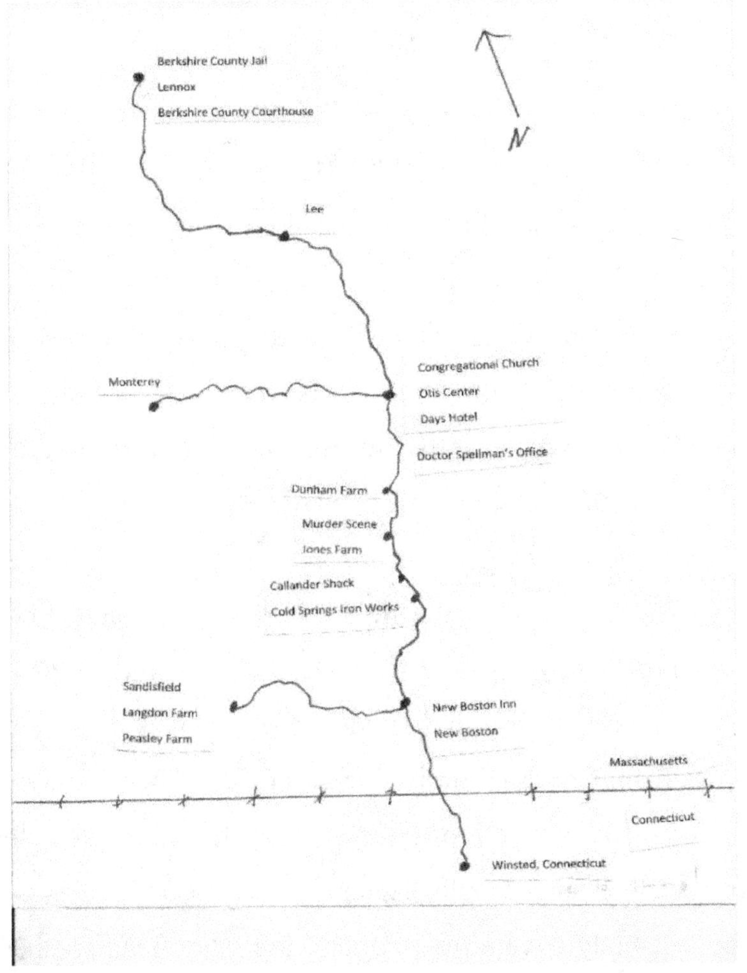

N
Berkshire County Jail
Lennox
Berkshire County Courthouse
Lee
Congregational Church
Monterey
Otis Center
Days Hotel
Doctor Spellman's Office
Dunham Farm
Murder Scene
Jones Farm
Callander Shack
Cold Springs Iron Works
Sandisfield
New Boston Inn
Langdon Farm
New Boston
Peasley Farm
Massachusetts
Connecticut
Winsted, Connecticut

Chapter One

Monday, September 8, 1862

Jones's Farm Pasture

Otis-Sandisfield Road

Otis, Massachusetts

6:00 PM

Sherriff Wesley Langdon had seen many things in his life, especially in his five years as a Deputy Sherriff of Berkshire County. His body tensed as he took in the gruesome scene before him. This was going to test his composure. Farmers, searching for the better part of a day and a half for a missing family in the Cold Spring section of Otis, had located human remains in a local pasture. They led Wesley to a corner of the field where several large trees, brought down by a summer thunderstorm, formed a tangle of branches and crushed underbrush. It was here they showed him three partially buried bodies. They had been there for some time, emanating a horrific odor. Near the outer edge of this tangle, under a fallen tree trunk, was a woman's body covered with dried blood, her head crushed, disfiguring horribly. Wesley sucked his breath in and felt the sweat forming on his forehead. No sooner had he taken in that grisly scene when his gaze was pulled a few feet more inside the tangle by the buzz of flies swarming over the bloodied bodies of two tiny souls. The missing children. He didn't need to get closer to see that their heads were so crushed that they almost ceased to exist.

In an instant, his mind flashed back to the last time he had seen a dead child, his own. His beautiful wife Rachael clutched their stillborn daughter, childbirth gone wrong; both dead, their blank eyes staring upward, just before they nailed the coffin's lid shut. This raw memory, coupled with the flies and the smell, caused his head to spin, threatening his equilibrium, while his violently churning gut quickly overpowered his self-resolve. He quickly turned away, retching as he went.

When he finally stopped heaving, he wiped his chin clean with his hand and looked up to see several farmers staring blankly at him. This … certainly wasn't gaining their confidence.

Sherriff Wesley Langdon, a farmer himself from Sandisfield, was a few months short of 33 years old, rugged and weathered from his battles with the Berkshire dirt; well, less dirt, more rock. He stood only 5'10" tall but was solid at 225 pounds. He had more schooling than most folks, 12 years in a one-room schoolhouse, and read constantly.

He had applied for the Deputy Sheriffs' job to supplement his farm income some five years prior. No, he admitted to himself, that was a lie. He had to escape the empty house after his family's death. He had literally thrown himself into the Deputy Sherriff's job. The county had provided some training, giving him books to read and some lessons from local lawyers before they swore him in. The meager training had stirred his interest in the art of investigations and law practice. He felt confident, which showed in his carriage, an important asset for anyone involved with people and enforcing the law. His investigative experience to date consisted of land and neighbor disputes, farmer complaints like cows being milked at night, livestock rustling, and miscellaneous thefts. His most prominent case was a burglary at the New Boston Inn, which he quickly solved when the drunk burglar dropped his billfold at the scene. Common sense had served him well, giving him confidence in his abilities. Now that confidence seemed sadly misplaced, facing this mess. With a sudden shutter, he also realized that he was the only man in a position to get justice for this family.

A commotion among the onlookers gathered on the Otis-Sandisfield Road caught his attention. A middle-aged, well-dressed man was making his way toward the sheriff. Wesley noted he was somewhat overweight and didn't have the muscular stride of a well-worked farm hand.

Wesley stepped out to meet him. "Sherriff," the man said, extending his arm to shake hands, "Doctor H. Spellman," he puffed, out of breath. "The search party sent for me. I'm the local Doctor and know most of these people. I suppose they feel comforted with me being here,"

Wesley knew of Dr. Spellman but had never met the man before.

Spellman continued almost apologetically. "If you don't mind a medical observation Sherriff, you look terrible."

Wesley didn't mince words, "Here's why."

He took the Doctor by the elbow, led him to the brush tangle, and pointed. The Doctor looked, his face blanching, his legs giving out, causing him to fall to his knees. "Oh God, who could do this?" the Doctor hissed, unable to breathe.

"That's what I, with your help, good doctor, have to find out."

"What can I do to help," the Doctor asked through clenched teeth.

Wesley took charge. "You get a couple of these folks to help you cut this brush out of your way and examine the bodies. Identify them if you can. We probably already know who they are, but we must do this one step at a time. Look for anything that could have been used as a weapon, footprints, or any sign that could help identify who did this. If you find anything, ensure it isn't messed with and send one of the farmers to get me. Remember, we can't assume anything. Whoever did this can't be let to get away with it."

Wesley organized a few men to help the Doctor and then made his way back across the pasture, where several other local farmers from the search party had gathered at his request. His thoughts were swirling. What a world it was, he thought. The Civil War was raging down to the South; men were dying by the thousands, and families were being shattered. Damn it, life was getting way too cheap! Killing was becoming a common way of life.

He shrugged off these thoughts as he approached the group of farmers. He nodded to men he knew. They were good men dressed roughly in wool, work clothes, mostly homemade. He recognized the patched clothes as a mark of the hard knocks farming the Berkshires inflicted. He could trust these men. He felt it instinctually.

Wesley walked to where the search party was gathered. "Men, we need to search this field. Did anyone see anything during their search earlier that might tell us where these folks were killed?"

One of the searchers, the teenage son of a local farmer, stepped forward. "I saw a little blood over the other side of the pasture. I just thought someone potted a rabbit. Was' fore I knew anyone was dead."

"Good," replied Wesley. "We start there. Anybody got anything else I should know?"

Another searcher stepped forward. Wesley recognized him as a local farmer, "Don't know iffen it means anything sheriff. A couple of sports fishin in the pond, top of the hill," he indicated with the wave of an arm, "stopped as they were leavin' and asked about the commotion. When I told 'em bout it, they said they were camping and fishin' round Cotton Pond last two days. I asked them if they had seen anything strange. Said the only thing they saw out of the ordinary was early Sunday mornin'. They saw a young colored guy walking by the pond down the hill in this direction."

Wesley's interest peeked, "You know who they were? Where were they from? I sure would like to talk to them."

"Nope, never saw em before. Went south towards Sandisfield. Maybe staying down there at the Inn."

"Ok, I'll look into that later. Right now, we're fighting dark. "You," indicating the searcher who had reported the blood, "take us over to where you saw the blood," ordered Wesley.

The group moved across the pasture. It was mostly ankle high but in places higher than that. The rough native grasses were interspersed with low bush blackberries laced with thorns along the vines that grabbed at their boots, threatening to trip them. They arrived at the spot the searcher indicated, and indeed there was a small stain on the ground that could be blood. It was about 400 yards north from where the bodies had been discovered.

Wesley directed the searchers to fan out from the blood and scour the ground. It wasn't but a few minutes when he heard a shout from closer to the bodies. He went over to find a searcher standing over a bucket partially filled with blackberries. The bucket was on the ground, tipped over, berries spilling out. In addition to the berries, a woman's bonnet, a very small boy's cap, and a few pairs of different stockings and shoes were stuffed into the bucket.

"Looks like this is the right area, boys. Concentrate around here." Wesley directed.

Wesley picked up the bucket and its contents to take with him. Maybe someone would know if it was from the missing family.

A few minutes later, another shout beckoned Wesley to an area of the pasture where a stone wall separated the pasture edge from the woods. The wall was short, only a rock or two tall. The searcher pointed out dark stains on several rocks that looked out of place sitting atop the wall. Wesley knelt to look more closely and recoiled violently.

Along the back of the wall, in the area of the stains, he saw bits of what looked like, to his untrained eye, bone with hair and blood... he couldn't describe what he was seeing other than stuff, maybe skin, hanging from them. He recovered and gently moved the bushes aside. There was a good deal more of the gory mess, much of it hanging close to the ground on the blackberry vines. It had the odor of rotting meat about it. Was this what was left of the children's heads? The thought caused him to pause. He realized he needed the Doctor's medical knowledge to identify what he was seeing.

"You men, mark this spot with three sticks tied in a teepee. It's getting dark — time to quit for now. We don't want to tromp on something important. I'll come back in the morning with the Doc."

When they were done, Wesley called the search party together. He sighed and said gently, "You folks are good friends and neighbors. I know this was tough for you to see. Go to your homes and hug your families. Remember what you saw here. Life is just too short." He shook each man's hand in turn, then started back down and across the hill to confer with the Doctor.

Darkness fell fast now. Wesley tripped several times on the tangle of underbrush and blackberry vines before he reached the Doctor. In the fading twilight, he saw that the Doctor had organized the farmers. They had removed the bulk of the brush, exposing the bodies. The Doctor knelt next to the two smaller bodies, perhaps thirty inches tall.

Wesley summoned the Doctor over to where he stood, not wanting to get any closer to the carnage than necessary. "Well, Doc, what do you think?"

The Doctor sighed deeply. "I can tell you a couple of things now, but I want to get them back to my place for a better look. The woman is Emily Jones, George's wife. That's about all I can tell you for sure. A quick exam tells me she was killed by several blows to the head. Her dress and underclothes were pulled up, almost over her head. I checked, and there is bruising, tearing with cuts, and scratches consistent with what I would expect to see with forcible rape. The two younger bodies, I believe, are her son George, aged three, and her daughter Sarah, aged two. I delivered both kids, but I can't identify them for sure. Their heads were beaten so severely. The features of their faces are just… gone. The beating they took was vicious. I can also tell you they weren't killed where they found them. Parts of the kid's skulls, face, hair and a lot of blood are missing. I… I just don't know."

Wesley replied, "We may have found the area where they were killed. I need you to look at what I found. We will get to that tomorrow."

Wesley looked back toward the bodies. "Doc, we should wait for the coroner." He looked up at the gathering darkness. "Well hell, it's getting dark. We can't wait or leave em here. Make notes on everything and take the bodies back to your place. I need you to meet me here at about an hour after dawn tomorrow. Later tomorrow, you can do a better exam on the bodies. He paused, "You all set? Got all the help you need?"

The Doctor simply nodded.

Wesley turned on his heel and left the Doctor to his awful business.

He headed across the bottom corner of the pasture toward the Jones's farmhouse, a dim glow from the lights within guiding his way. He was still a long way from supper and bed, although he doubted sleep would come easy after what he had witnessed today.

Chapter Two

Monday, September 8, 1862

The Jones's Farmhouse

Otis, Massachusetts

8:00 PM

Wesley made his way to the Jones's farmhouse. It sat about an eighth of a mile south of where the bodies were discovered. The door was wide open. His eyes adjusted slowly to the gloomy interior, the light provided by smoky oil lamps. He saw three men sitting on chairs around a roughly hewn kitchen table. All three had their heads down, and one was sobbing uncontrollably.

Wesley approached and introduced himself to the trio. "I'm Wesley Langdon, Deputy Sherriff Berkshire County. Who is George Jones?"

The sobbing man looked up, trying to speak, but the attempt failed. One of the other two men said," Sherriff can't this wait? He just found out his family is dead."

Wesley spoke strongly, "No, it can't. Time is important here. Now you two out… and shut the door behind you. I want to talk to George alone." The two men hesitantly rose and stalked out of the house.

Wesley looked closely at George Jones. He was young, Wesley guessed twenty-five or so, with neatly cut, sandy blonde hair. He was medium height but slim and didn't exhibit the muscled body nor the callouses on his hands that came with farming the Berkshires. He was well dressed, the patched woolen farm clothes not in evidence. He looked more like a preacher than a farmer and seemed almost out of place in the farmhouse.

Wesley opened the conversation with a question. "George, you want to catch this guy or not?"

George Jones slowly raised his head, looked at Wesley, and nodded. "Tell me how," he sobbed, gradually gaining some control.

Wesley knew he had to be gentle but firm. He also learned from his reading that in most cases where a wife is murdered, her husband is guilty.

"George, tell me what happened. The last time you saw your wife and everything that happened since you last saw her."

Jones looked up, took a deep breath, and started. "Yesterday, ah… Sunday morning; you know we both usually go to church; I'm a church elder on the board there. Sunday… she didn't want to go. I really couldn't understand why she wouldn't go to church. She just said no. She wanted to pick berries instead. Something about making the kids something sweet and the berries being about gone for the season. She adored her kids. I'm ashamed to say that I didn't pay attention to her reasons for not attending church." Jones's composure threatened to break down.

Wesley interrupted softly," George, calm down and tell me the story."

"She was set on staying home, so I didn't argue. I went to the Congregational Church in Otis at about 9:30. Far as I know, she went berry picking with the two kids. I got back from church at about 5:00 PM, and she wasn't home. That wasn't unusual; she was free-spirited. It wasn't unusual for her to see something, an animal, waterfall, or whatnot, and wander off to show the kids and spend time with them. She often would walk the mile to her parent's farm, visit them on a whim."

George paused, "Anyway, I went back for evening services at 6:30 PM, getting home around 9:00 PM. They still were not home. I was worried and went to her parent's farm, but she wasn't there. Her dad and I got several neighbors to help look for them. We searched until midnight, gave up, and started again at dawn. More folks joined us Monday morning, and we searched until just after 4 PM. You know what theee…," he dissolved back into sobbing tears, unable to continue.

Wesley picked up the bucket still containing a few blackberries and other clothing items that he had found in the field and put it on the table. "George, please, try to get ahold of yourself; we got work to do. Is this your bucket?"

Jones looked up, squinting through tear-filled eyes. "That's our kitchen bucket. We keep it in the kitchen, keep it clean, and use it for food, like vegetables from the garden, eggs from the henhouse, or wild stuff we pick. Where did you find it?"

"That's not important right now, George. Would your wife take it to pick blackberries?"

"Yes."

Wesley removed the items inside; George immediately grabbed them and held them to his chest and began sobbing. Finally, he held out the bonnet and told Wesley it was his wife's. He identified various other clothing items as his son's or daughter's. His grief kept him from talking in complete sentences.

"George, I got to ask this, so don't get upset. Who can tell me that you were at church that whole time you said you were?"

"You think I killed my wife? My kids?" he shouted as he stood up and faced the Sherriff, his face beet red.

"Sit down," Wesley flatly stated, taking command of the moment. "We have to do this right. Who can vouch for you?"

"I was in church with twenty-five other people. Ask them if you don't believe me. Services were over at about noon. The board meeting started right after that. There were six of us, along with Rev Thomas Hall, the pastor, at that meeting. That lasted till 4:30, and then I came straight home. I got home at about five. I was home alone till about 6:30 when I returned to church for evening services. I was there with the reverend and others in the congregation till about 8:30. I came directly home. Was here by 9:00 PM, you know the rest."

"First of all, George, it's not a question of whether I believe you," Wesley explained. "I have to know… to check. That's how we do these things. Listen, when you were here alone, between 5:00 PM and 6:30 PM, what did you do for that hour and a half?"

"Sherriff, I know what you're thinking, but I never saw anyone during that time. I fed the chickens and other livestock and made a light supper of cheese, bread, and cured ham. Look! The dishes are still in the sink. Then it was time to head back to church. I loved my family. I couldn't hurt them!"

"George, I got to ask this too. It's going to upset you, but I gotta ask. How was your marriage?"

"You son of a bitch! I ought to turn you inside out. That's none of your business."

"Calm down, George. I told you I gotta ask."

"My marriage was great." George answered almost defensively, "We got married four years ago. The kids came along… we were happy!"

That answer didn't convince Wesley. It almost sounded as if George was trying to convince himself everything was good. Wesley could see George losing his composure and debated questioning him further but realized it was useless. He had gotten what he needed for now.

"George, I will be back tomorrow to talk more. Try and get some rest; the best thing for you right now. Believe me, I know."

With that, Wesley turned, walking out of the house… it certainly wasn't a home any longer. He knew that from personal experience. He waved Jones' friends back into the house and started down the hill to check on the Doctor's progress.

Chapter Three

Monday, September 8, 1862

On the Otis-Sandisfield Road by the Jones Farm

Otis, Massachusetts

9:00 PM

Wesley walked away from the farmhouse toward several lights which were visible along Otis-Sandisfield Road. When he reached the road, he discovered the visible lights were lanterns on the Doctor's buckboard. The Doctor and several local farmers were securing one larger and two smaller bundles wrapped in blankets in the back of the buckboard. Wesley sighed deeply. They had to be the bodies. The Doctor looked exhausted and wore an anguished look on his face. He appeared much older than he had a few hours before.

"Sherriff, we are both exhausted. It's late, and my place is fifteen minutes up the road. The wife will have supper on the stove. You can stay there the night; it's closer than your place in Sandisfield. You can get back here quicker in the morning, and we can compare notes."

Wesley considered this for a moment. A home-cooked meal and conversation would be nice. "Doc, I'd love to take you up on that, but I got a lot of things to mull over. I want to make some notes while things are fresh in my mind, plus I want to stop at the New Boston Inn and see if those fishermen that stopped might be staying there. They could leave early in the morning, and I don't want to lose any information. Tell you what, I'll meet you here about 8 AM tomorrow."

The Doctor stroked his chin and said, "Ok Sherriff, you get some rest. These folks," a sweep of the hand indicating the wrapped bodies, "are gonna need you rested and sharp."

"Goes for you too, Doc. Good night."

With that, Wesley turned and used the light from the Doctor's buggy to tighten his saddle cinch, then mounted his horse and turned south along the road towards Sandisfield and his farm.

The horse knew the road and was eager to be home, trotting along without guidance, the leather from the saddle creaking in time with the horse's cadence. The warm night air coupled with all these things, allowed Wesley's mind to wander. What did he know for sure? What didn't he know? He must have dozed off in the saddle and was shocked to see the lights of Sandisfield through the trees so quickly. He pulled up at the New Boston Inn, tied his horse to the hitch out front, and entered the Inn. The dining room was empty, but loud voices came from the taproom.

He entered the taproom and recognized Daniel Brown Jr., the proprietor, talking to several men with beer mugs in front of them. Daniel looked up and greeted him warmly.

"Sherriff, you look beat. Supper? Heard there was a murder up Cold Springs way."

Wesley sat heavily on one of the bar stools. "Yeah, bad stuff. Daniel, you got any stew left?"

"Sure thing. I'll heat some up. Beer?" Daniel replied.

Wesley sighed tiredly, "Sounds good, but I need some information right now. Some fishermen stopped by and talked to the farmers helping me out. I guess they were fishing up Cotton Pond way. They said they saw a negro boy headed down the hill toward Cold Spring on Sunday. You got any fishermen staying the night?

Before Daniel could answer, one of the men at the bar spoke up. "We were them fishermen Sherriff. Yeah, we have seen a light-skinned colored boy, maybe 20 or so, about 8- 9 Sunday morning. We yelled at him cause he had used one of our boats. He left quick like without sayin much."

Wesley asked, "You said light-skinned about 20?"

"Yup. He was too far to see much, but he was surely light skinned."

The other three men shook their heads in agreement.

"Can you tell me anything else?"

"Sorry, Sherriff, we were more interested in the fishing."

"Thanks, guys; it's more than I knew five minutes ago."

Daniel brought a bowl of steaming stew and set that and a mug of cold beer in front of Wesley. "Sherriff, you need this after the day you had. It's on me."

Wesley simply nodded his thanks.

The meal hit the spot, and the beer started to relax Wesley. He ate in silence, listening to the fishing tales of the others.

The atmosphere at the Inn was comfortable, but he knew he had to go. He was dozing off and desperately needed some sleep. At about 11:15 PM, he said his goodbyes and headed to his place.

The farmhouse was cold, dark, and lonely. He went about the chores of taking care of his horse, starting a fire in the stove, and lighting some oil lanterns. Finally, he fell into bed at about midnight. Sleep, surprisingly, came quickly; It was daylight before he knew it.

Chapter Four

Tuesday, September 9, 1862

Farmhouse of Deputy Sherriff Wesley Langdon,

Sandisfield, Massachusetts

6:30 AM

Wesley stretched as he stood before the wood-fired kitchen stove, making coffee, eggs, and hard tack, for breakfast. He looked out the window and silently lamented how his farm had deteriorated over the last few years. The barn needed paint, the house was filthy, and the fences needed mending. He had forsaken most of his livestock, butchering some and selling others. He wondered if his heart would ever truly be in it again. He was spending almost all his time being a sheriff rather than a farmer. Soon as this case was behind him, he promised himself he would spend more time on the farm. Reluctantly, he turned his attention to breakfast and the day ahead.

After doing his breakfast dishes, Wesley went out to the barn, the morning air crisp and fresh. Summer was quickly fading toward fall. He fed, watered, brushed, and saddled his horse before riding out into the morning air. The ride to Otis was directly along the banks of the Farmington River, and the contrast in temperatures between air and water caused a plume of mist to rise off it. The mist intermittently flowed over the road, and riding into and out of it gave the road an almost supernatural appearance; appropriate, Wesley thought since he was dealing with death.

It was almost 8 AM, with the warming sun beginning to dissipate the mist, when Wesley arrived at the Jones' farm in Cold Spring. The good Doctor was already there, waiting patiently on his buckboard. Wesley noted he was not dressed in his "doctor's clothes" as he had been the day before but had rougher, working clothes on. It was apparent he was ready to get dirty if need be. Wesley nodded approvingly to the Doctor and received a simple nod back.

The Doctor followed Wesley up the lane to the Jones farm. When they reached the farmhouse, they both dismounted. There was no light or activity evident from the house.

The Doctor had a black leather bag in hand and said simply, "Lead on, Sheriff."

They walked across the pasture, their pant legs soaked from the dew adhering to the grasses. The teepee the searchers had erected the previous night, which marked the area where they had discovered blood, was like a beacon across the pasture. They stopped short of the marker where the first stain was still apparent on the ground.

Wesley started, "Doc, look at this stain on the ground. Blood?" The Doctor looked closely.

He replied, "I think so. Where is the other blood and tissue you told me about?"

Wesley led the pair to the rock wall. "Look here. Behind the wall in the low underbrush."

The Doctor bent down and looked. "Hummm," was his only remark. He opened his bag and took out a small pail and a plyer-like tool.

He used this to pick up the bone fragments and other bloody remains and place them in the small pail. It was all unidentifiable to Wesley. The Doctor continued in silence for several minutes before looking up.

"Sherriff, this was where I believe the kids were killed. The skull bones and skin fragments are consistent with the damage I observed to their faces yesterday. The other bloodstain", he pointed back to the smaller stain, "I can't say. Let me finish up here. You can go on to whatever else you got to do. Meet me at my place afternoon; I'll probably have something to tell you then."

Wesley simply nodded and walked back to his horse. There was still no movement in or around the Jones farmhouse.

Wesley rode north to Otis Center, searching for Reverend Hall at the Congregational Church. They had much to discuss. The ride took about twenty minutes, which Wesley noted roughly fit the times in George's story. The Congregational Church was quiet when he arrived. When he inquired about Reverend Hall, a young lady sweeping the church's front steps directed him to the nearby parsonage.

A middle-aged lady answered his knock at the door and introduced herself as the housekeeper. She directed Wesley into a sitting room and asked him to wait while she located the Reverend. Wesley waited and glanced about him. The parsonage was a far cry from your typical Berkshire farmhouse. The walls were covered with luxurious wallpaper, and there were numerous expensive-looking paintings in ornate frames hung about the room.

The shiny wood floors were covered with lush rugs scattered about the room. The moldings around the door casings, floors, and ceilings were not your standard milled board but ornated carved woodwork. Wesley had been to Boston once in his life and had seen houses like this. They oozed money and prestige, almost societal dishonesty, as opposed to the honest simplicity of a farmhouse.

The Reverend's entrance fit the aura of the sitting room. He was tall, over 6'3", and rail thin. His neatly pressed black outfit hung loosely on his thinness while his bright white collar seemed overly snug on his neck. Wesley noted that his face was thin, and his nose pointed like the beak of a bird of prey. When the Reverend looked at you, he appeared to sight down that beak, not unlike a hunter down the barrel of his gun. The totality of his personage suggested a prim and proper man, exuding a self-possessed authority.

The silence was deafening as they sized each other up. Wesley broke it by introducing himself. "I'm Wesley

Langdon, Deputy Sherriff Berkshire County. I'm investigating the murder of Emily Jones and her children."

In answer, the Reverend pulled a pair of spectacles from his breast pocket and a handkerchief from a hip pocket and began polishing his glasses vigorously. "What can I do for you, Sherriff?"

Wesley was confounded by the Reverend's actions. The rubbing of the glasses appeared to him as almost a ruse or distraction to the words he actually spoke. This man was not to be trifled with. Carefully he moved on. "Reverend, how well do you know the family?"

"I've known George Jones since he was a very young man and his folks for years before that. He is an upright Christian man and a dedicated resource to this congregation. I would do anything for that man as he would do for this church. He is truly on God's path to salvation. His wife, on the other hand," he hesitated, "was not a Congregationalist, although George, and those in the congregation, tried their best to convert her to God's way. She was, how do I say this properly, a free-spirited and a free-thinking woman, certainly not within God's grace."

Confused, Wesley said," Reverend, you will have to explain that last remark."

The spectacles came out with the handkerchief, and the polishing began again. Finally, he answered, "Sherriff, we Congregationalists are very serious about our religion and our relationship with God. God requires certain things of us. Things like attending services and devotion to God through other actions, such as participating in the congregation, are mandatory. She was taught these things but made a conscious decision to ignore them. Therefore, she was, in our eyes, outside of God's grace."

"I take it you were not fond of her."

"I suppose she was a good enough person. You must take into consideration my position here. I am the pastor of a small flock of Congregationalists. I can only care for the spiritual needs of my congregation, for they own the kingdom of heaven. I care not what others think. My measurement of success is what God will think of my flock on judgement day. My entire being must go into that mission. She was beyond my caring if she did not want to be in that congregation."

Wesley was shocked by the uncaring, segregationist attitude of the Reverend but persevered in his line of questioning. "How was their marriage? You sound like you were close to George."

The Reverend repeated the ritual of rubbing his glasses, then replied. "I married them. George was young, and she was the first woman who turned his head. He couldn't believe a pretty girl like Emily would consent to spend her life with him. George assumed she would follow him and enter our congregation as would any good wife. She obviously had very different ideas. She was, how would you put it, free-spirited. Organized religion seemed not for her. By the time George realized this, they had their first child, and it was too late. George came to me very upset. I told him time would take care of this. That advice may have been overly optimistic."

"Reverend, I need to know if George was here at Church last Sunday when he was here and if you noticed anything strange about his behavior."

Off came the glasses, and out came the handkerchief; the glasses were again polished to a high sheen as the Reverend seemed to stall. He finally answered, "Sherriff, George was here from about 10 AM until 4:30 PM. He left and returned for evening prayers at 7 PM and left about 8:30. I was either with him or saw him during those times." The glasses returned to the hawk-like nose, the handkerchief to the pocket. With a gaze down that beak of a nose, he continued," George was upset Sunday morning that Emily and the children didn't accompany him to services as required." The reverend emphasized the word required. "He spoke to me about it, and said he was confused by her behavior.

I counseled him to be patient with her, but I can tell you he was very upset with her. I still held out hope that she might respond to God's call." He paused, "I know you think George could be responsible for this, but I can tell you George takes God's word seriously. God commands; thou shalt not kill. Thus George could not kill anyone, let alone his wife and children. You need to look elsewhere."

"Reverend, this is important. What was George like when he came back for evening prayers? Was he agitated or disheveled, more so than when he left at 4:30?"

The Reverend's hands went for his glasses and handkerchief but stopped short of his usual ritual. He started slowly, "I know what you're looking for, Sherriff. I must tell you George was fine when he arrived at 7:00 PM. I can't imagine George would hurt Emily and surely not the kids. He simply adored the children no matter what he thought of Emily's lack of faith. In spite of his religious zeal, he had no plans of leaving his wife and family. I often worried, if forced to choose, he would have forsaken the promise of heaven before wrecking his family."

Wesley looked up and noted the man seemed sincere in his statements. "Reverend, I appreciate your frankness. Can you think of anything that will help me out here?"

The Reverend paused, "I think you should speak to Emily's father, Gamaliel Dunham. She was very close to her folks. Get their take on things. It might give you more insight. Emily certainly did not confide in me."

Wesley thanked the Reverend and bade his farewell. He pulled himself into the saddle and headed south to the good Doctor's office on the south end of town. During the short ride, he reviewed his conversation with the Reverend. No doubt he supported George and wasn't that fond of Emily. Yet despite the religious chip on his shoulder, his answers seemed truthful and more importantly, corroborated George's story — time to move on.

Wesley pulled his pocket watch out and noted it was only 10:30 AM. Too early to go to the Doctor. He continued south past the Doctor's home to the Dunham farm.

Chapter Five

Tuesday, September 9, 1862

The Dunham Family Farm

Otis-Sandisfield Road

Otis, Massachusetts

10:45 AM

Wesley found the Dunham family farm without difficulty. It was between Otis Center and the Jones farm off the Otis-Sandisfield Road. At first glance, it was a typical, small Berkshire farm. It consisted of a house, barn, and a few other outbuildings, not unlike his, all sadly in need of a coat of paint. In spite of that, it all seemed in good repair, and the farm was clean and tidy. A cow mooed loudly from the barn, and the comforting sounds of chickens clucking and cooing as they fed in the barnyard supplied background noise. The farm dog barked at him as he rode up, dismounted, and tied his horse to a stunted, gnarly apple tree outside the barn. In response to the dog, an older man exited the barn wiping his hands on an old rag he was carrying. He was dressed in the uniform of a Berkshire farmer, patched, handmade, woolen clothes with a worn hat worn loosely over his head. He walked bent over with a slight limp as if age, work, and life had placed too much weight on his shoulders.

Wesley walked up to the man and introduced himself. "Mr. Dunham, I'm Deputy Sherriff Wesley Langdon. Do you have a few minutes to talk?"

Dunham shook Wesley's hand with a firm grip while looking him up and down, all the time working a wad of chewing tobacco around his mouth. "Guess it's got to be. You know what bastard did this? I got my shotgun loaded in the house!"

Wesley nodded, sensing the man's anger. "Not yet, and I need your help. Reverend Hall suggested we talk."

"That pompous ass." Dunham spits a big load of tobacco juice on the ground. "He has done more to cause this than anybody. If George had spent more time farming and husbanding than in that church, he would have been there to protect my little girl and the grandkids."

Wesley paused, surprised by the depth of his hatred. "Mr. Dunham, exactly how much time did George spend at the church?"

"He would go every day for at least a few hours instead of taking care of his family. Emily told me she did most of the farm chores and took care of the house and kids because of his church time. She wouldn't have anything to do with that church or that homewrecker of a Reverend. She told me that plain as day."

"Mr. Dunham, be that as it may, what I really need to know is who had a beef with your daughter bad enough to do this? You think George did it?"

Mr. Dunham guffawed loudly, "That boy got no backbone," spitting tobacco juice to the side. "No, he didn't do it. You didn't see his face when he came stormin up here Sunday night. No, he couldn't do it. Now you want to look somewhere? You go down by the Sandisfield line to that black bastard's house, one with his white wife. They got so many kin and half kin in and out all the time, you can't keep count, and they got no farm, no animals, no food. They're stealing animals all the time so they don't starve. Emily told me she was sure the youngest son would sneak into their barn at night and milk their cow. She'd go out to milk most mornings, and the cow was dry. She was complaining about em all the time."

"Do you know the name of that family?"

"Naw, I think it's something like Collender, but I ain't sure. Ain't but one colored family in Otis. Think they do coal haulin for the Iron Forge."

"Can you think of anyone else with that much hate against your daughter?"

"Sherriff, she was carefree and happy. I don't know anyone else who would want to hurt her, nor a reason why. All I know is she's gone." His anguish shown clearly through the tough veneer.

There was little else to say. Wesley promised to do his best and catch the guy who killed his daughter. Then he mounted up and headed back to Otis to see the Doctor. As he rode along, he pondered this new information. He was familiar with this colored family with the white wife Dunham had mentioned.

He had been there on several occasions when neighboring farmers complained animals were missing and had insinuated the black family was responsible. They were a slick bunch. Not once had Wesley found enough evidence to arrest them. What Dunham had said had a ring of truth. There was a constant parade of colored relatives staying with the family, including many young colored men with no local roots. This, Wesley thought, might tie in with what the fisherman saw on the morning of the murder. He pushed that thought to the back of his mind as the Doctor's home came into sight.

He arrived at the Doctor's office just about noon. He noted the Doctor's buckboard plus another sturdier, newer one tied next to it. He tied his horse to the hitching post and entered the office. Dr. Spellman was talking to another well-dressed man. Spellman looked up as he entered, greeting him warmly. "Sherriff, officialdom has caught up with us, I'm afraid. The Berkshire County Coroner, Dr. Parsons, is here to help with my examination."

Dr. Parsons stepped forward and shook Wesley's hand. "The good doctor here sings your praises, Sherriff; says you are doing a standup job with this dirty business."

"That's embarrassing. I have nothing so far," Wesley countered.

"I have a letter from your boss, Sherriff Root. He asked me to give it to you personally and convey any response you see fit to submit."

Wesley took the letter and put it in his pocket. He had never had a reason to meet Doctor Parsons before. Parsons was older than Doctor Spellman but carried himself with a carriage that reminded Wesley more of the city and the officialdom Doctor Spellman had referred to. His white hair was receding, and this, combined with thick glasses and ample girth, gave him the look of a teacher or professor rather than a physician. In spite of this, he exuded a feeling of sincerity and warmth. You felt he wanted to be involved, not fearing work and trying to find the truth. Wesley couldn't put his finger on it but instantly trusted the man.

"What can you fine doctors tell me?"

The two doctors smiled at him, and Dr. Parsons said, "First lunch, this good country doctor has got a wife that can cook like a French chef." With that, the two doctors led him to an attached home where a large spread of food was laid out.

The threesome ate, exchanging pleasantries as they chewed. Wesley grew to like Parsons as they talked. He felt his initial instinct about the coroner was correct. He was down to earth and seemed to possess a farmer's common sense.

The food was delicious. It had been a long time since someone had cooked for him; he instantly regretted not accepting Doctor Spellman's invitation from the night before. After the food was gone, the three men relaxed over coffee. Although the mood was relaxed, the substance of the visit hung over them like a dark cloud.

Dr. Parsons opened the conversation: "Sherriff, we finished our exam of all three bodies. We are united in our opinions." Dr. Spellman nodded in agreement. Parsons continued. "Emily Jones, the mother, was raped, probably more than once, judging from the bruising and tearing involved. She was killed by multiple blows to the front of her head. They impacted her face and skull. I can't tell what the weapon was. The depressions in her skull were rounded, if that helps. It could have been anything. There were wounds to the back of the head, but they were much less severe. Her head was probably on a hard surface when the frontal blows were delivered. That's only our opinion, but that appears to be the best explanation as to the cause of the damage to the back of her head. Any questions, Sherriff?"

Wesley simply shook his head to the negative.

Dr. Parsons continued, "The two children were a different story. They had bruising around their ankles as if someone held their ankles and swung them around, like a rag doll or a scythe. Whoever did it hit their heads repeatedly against a solid surface, literally beating their brains out."

Dr. Spellman broke in, "I think it was that rock wall at the pasture edge. Think about it, Sherriff; you discovered it. If someone, and they would have to be fairly strong, grabbed the kids by the ankles and swung them in a circle striking their heads again and again against those rocks, the force of the spinning would have spread the skull fragments, skin, and eventually the brains into the brush beyond the wall. That's exactly where and how we found those human remains."

Dr. Parsons added, "It was a brutal killing." What I think we can tell you is that the killer or killers, there could be more than one and they were well-muscled males. They raped the mother and killed the kids to keep them quiet, not necessarily in that order. Too much time went by before we found the bodies even to guess a time of death."

Dr. Spellman sighed deeply, "One more bit of information Sherriff, the mother's head wounds had bits of her skirt and underclothes in the wounds as if she was struck in the head through the clothing. They probably raped her and then killed her immediately. Remember, her skirt was still over her head when we found her. No real defensive wounds, only a few scratches. Are you following me, Sherriff?"

Wesley thought a moment, then nodded. "There is a lot of information here. I see at least three different scenarios regarding how it happened. The first was the mother was raped and killed first — no defensive wounds which fit. But probably unlikely since the kids would have put up a racket and had to be contained before being killed. How could one person do that?"

The second option was the kids were killed first, which would mean the mother would be screaming and fighting as only a mother could. Again, how could one person handle all that? Again, no defensive wounds on the mother. Doesn't make sense. Somebody would likely have heard something in either of those two cases."

The third option seems most likely to me. There were two or more attackers, one handling the mother and the other taking care of the kids. That way less noise and less chance of being seen or heard. They raped and killed the mother and the kids almost simultaneously. Either way, there was a lot of hate in this thing."

The two doctors nodded as one. Parsons explained, "Your observations seem absolutely correct given the wounds. You need to find someone that hated them, or just her, so much so that they felt the need to kill her and two defenseless children. The person, or persons, who did this must have little regard for human life, and because of that, I would bet they have committed other crimes. I believe you might have had dealings with him or them in the past, Sherriff."

Wesley thought about this and realized the facts seemed to be pointing him in a definite direction. He thanked the doctors and excused himself to read the letter from his boss. High Sherriff Root, Sherriff of Berkshire County, was, above all, a politician, but in spite of this, Wesley had always found him to be fair and reasonable. Wesley really didn't know what to expect. The letter said,

Deputy Sherriff Langdon,

I have followed the news accounts and other reports on the incident down there in Otis. It appears you have everything under control. This incident is in the public eye and has become the talk of the town. It is important that the public feels we are protecting them. Therefore, we must catch, prosecute and punish the person who committed this unspeakable act sooner rather than later.

If you need any assistance, don't hesitate to get in touch with Deputy Sherriff Muncie in Monterey. I have instructed him to meet with you and offer any assistance you require with this case. Use him as you see fit.

I have complete confidence in you. I am sure I will hear of an arrest in this matter soon.

Sherriff A. Root

Wesley shook his head in disbelief. Root was running true to form. Votes were as important to him as solving the crime was. He reread the letter and thought about the strong suggestion from Root to take on help. He knew Muncie from past investigations and liked him, but his gut was telling him it would be simpler for him to continue the investigation himself. On the other hand, there were many minor witnesses to speak to and other loose ends that would eat up his time and keep him from the main line of the investigation. Wesley weighed the decision carefully and concluded that Muncie's assistance would be helpful.

Wesley penned a quick note to Sherriff Root, thanking him for the offer of help and promising to contact Muncie. He thanked the Sherriff for his confidence but stopped well short of promising a quick arrest. He assured Root he was working hard and had leads, then closed the note.

He went looking for Doctor Parsons to give him the note and found the two doctors still at the table dallying over dessert and more coffee. He declined the offer to join them, handing Parsons his reply to Sherriff Root. He made a sandwich for later, in case the day ran late on him, remembering the last day.

Before he left, Parsons spoke up, "Wesley, are you going to see George Jones today?"

Wesley replied, "Yes, that's my next stop. Why?

"Let him know we are done with the bodies of his family, and he can make his arrangements with his choice of undertaker. We are set to release the bodies."

Wesley promised to pass the message on. He bade goodbye to the doctors, promising to keep them updated, mounted his horse, and turned south along the road en route to speak to George Jones.

Chapter Six

Tuesday, September 9, 1862

In route to the Jones Farm

Otis-Sandisfield Road

Otis, Massachusetts

1:30 PM

Wesley spent the horse ride to the Jones farm rolling all he had learned over and over in his mind. Everyone he talked to seemed to vouch for George Jones, even his father-in-law, who had his problems with the boy. The doctors felt strongly that there had to be two assailants, and he had to agree, given the evidence they had uncovered. Those facts made him think that George Jones was probably not involved in the killings. Then again, there were the ninety minutes he was home, the night of the murder, without an alibi. Wesley felt he couldn't totally write him off as a suspect. It was up to George now. Wesley wondered how this talk would go.

Wesley turned off the main road and down the lane to the Jones Farm at about 2:00 PM. He pulled up in front of the farmhouse, dismounted, and tied up his horse. The farm was eerily quiet. He couldn't put a finger on it, but he sensed something was wrong. He started toward the house and was almost to the door when it was thrown open, causing Wesley to jump back, startled. Standing in the doorway was a disheveled George Jones.

It appeared as if he had just gotten out of bed. His hair was in a wild tangle, his eyes had black bags under them and were rimmed with red, and his clothes were unbuttoned and wrinkled. The look on his face was shocked was one of shock when his eyes settled on Wesley.

"Sherriff, what time is it? I can't believe I slept this late! I have so much to do. I have to go see Reverend Hall and plan the funerals. Oh my God, how could I do this?"

"George, calm down. The doctors have just finished their examination of the bodies. They wanted me to tell you that you can start the arrangements for the funerals. You didn't miss anything. What time did you get to sleep anyway?

"My friends thought a few shots of applejack would be good for me. I never drink. It must have really hit me. I think that was about two this morning. I woke up when I heard you ride up."

Wesley put his hand on George's shoulder. "George, let's go in, make some coffee, and talk."

Wesley went in and told George to wash up while he started a fire in the ice-cold cook stove, pumped water from the hand pump in the kitchen, and started boiling it for coffee. He checked the ice box, found some hard tack and eggs, and got to frying them. When George returned to the room, he looked much more put together, and his meal was almost ready. Wesley set the food down before him, and George ate voraciously. Wesley settled for a cup of coffee and waited until George finished his breakfast before speaking.

"George, I've talked to a lot of people since yesterday. Your story seems to check out just fine. Your pastor speaks well of you. On another note, I spoke to your father-in-law today. He told me Emily had problems with some colored folks just down the road. What can you tell me about that?"

"I had forgotten about that. Yes, Emily was convinced that colored trash was stealing stock, mostly lambs, from us. I had found gut piles and hides several times, always at the back of the property in the woods, but we couldn't prove those folks were responsible. Emily also caught the youngest boy from that family in our barn late at night a week or so ago. Emily actually slept out there a couple of nights a week, trying to catch them in the act. That was after finding the milk cow dry a couple of times a month. She was convinced it was the boy, and she was right. She told me he walked in with a bucket after midnight last week. She told me she was so mad she screamed at the boy until he ran away. Yeah, Emily was convinced the coloreds were stealing us blind, and she wasn't bashful in who she told."

"Had any of the colored folks ever sassed her back or threatened her, or for that matter you?"

"She never told me if they had. They never said anything to me ever. You think they might have done this to her Sherriff?"

"Just following up on information, George. Maybe something, or it might be nothing. What I need you to do is bury your family. Let me ask the questions. Ok?"

George sighed deeply, "That's going to be hard for sure. You have my word. I'll leave it to you."

Wesley thanked him and drained his cold coffee from his cup in one gulp. "I think it's time I visited these black folks." He got up, went out the door, mounted up, reigning in his horse, and turned south.

The shack where the colored family lived was only about a half mile down the road. Wesley remembered it from two previous visits when he had come searching for stolen livestock. It was little more than a farm outbuilding pressed into service by the owners of the iron forge to house their part-time help. Wesley remembered from his previous investigations that the forge owners had explained that they employed a steady parade of part-time laborers, some white, a few colored. They hauled coal to the forge. This shack, and a few others like them, was where they housed them.

Wesley reined up in front of the shack and noted it had deteriorated since the last time he was there. Someone had made a half-hearted attempt to patch the many holes in the walls. They had nailed boards this way and that, resulting in a mish-mashed pattern that had missed plenty of the holes they intended to cover. There was a whisper of smoke coming from the rusted stove pipe that threatened to topple from the roof at any time. No barn, garden, or livestock was visible, and no soul moved in Wesley's vision. Wesley was about to dismount when the only door swung open, and a rough-looking white woman stepped out. She was dressed in a tattered, dirty woolen dress with many patches on it and looked like she hadn't bathed in a month. Her hair was a wild tangle, and a few smears of stove ash were on one cheek. Wesley recognized her from his past visits as the white wife and mother of this black family.

The woman studied Wesley for a moment. "You're the Sherriff. I remember you. You here to accuse us of something we didn't do again?"

"Ma'am," Wesley started, tipping his hat, "I only want some information. Who lives here?"

The woman chuckled. "No offense, Sherriff, but why in tarnation should I tell you anything? We have to scratch out an existence in this mess of a house. Everyone accuses my husband and son of stealing from them, hardly ever prove nothin'. Nobody ever cares if we live or die. You know why, Sherriff? Cause I'm a white woman married to a black man. What's worse, in white people's eyes, than just the fact that my man and son are black? No, you'll get no information from me. You best be going."

Wesley didn't move or break eye contact with the woman. "Your neighbors are not accusing you of anything, ma'am. I'm investigating a murder just up the road. You get in the way of that investigation, and I'll have to arrest you and get my information anyway. I don't want to do that, but I have to do my job. I'll ask one more time. Who lives in this house?"

The woman bristled and then shook her head in resignation. "Don't make no, never mind. Ain't no justice for our kind anyway. Nobody gonna stand up for us. You'll just makeup stuff, railroad my men, and look like a hero. That's the justice we're used to. I can't change it. I live here with my husband Thomas and son James."

"You had visitors here over the last week or so?"

The woman looked at him and laughed out loud. "White folks see a group of colored people together and get scared. That it? Yeah, Sherriff. My husband's four sons from Winsted worked at the Iron Works last week. They stayed here with us and left to go home Sunday morning. They took the stage and flagged it down on the Otis-Sandisfield Road.

"You got their names?"

"Nelson Warner, Homer Dolphin, his brother Charles Dolphin and Willis White," the woman spit out with obvious contempt in her voice. "They were your colored gang." She laughed.

"What time did they get to the stage Sunday morning?"

"Hell, does it look like I own a watch? Sun was up about two hours when they walked to the road. Don't know what time the stage came by."

"Where are Thomas and James now?"

"Where the hell do you think? Breaking their backs hauling coal for pennies a day at the Iron Works. Just like every other weekday. Hell, Sherriff, I thought you looked like a smart man. Now I ain't so sure."

Wesley ignored the insult. "Were Thomas and James home here with you all day Sunday?"

"Sherriff, I work my fingers to the bone all day, every day. One day runs into the other. Hardly see the light of day outside this shack. I can't remember rightly, for sure. You'll have to ask them."

From the saddle, Wesley tipped his hat. "Thank you for your time, ma'am. Oh, by the way. I don't give a tinkerer's damn what color a person's skin is. I only care that they obey the law. Afternoon, Ma'am." Wesley turned the horse and rode out onto the Road.

Wesley turned south towards Sandisfield. He pulled out his watch and saw it was already 3:30 PM. He knew the stage stopped at the New Boston Inn at about 4:00 PM on its way south. He spurred his horse forward. He arrived at the Inn just before 4:00 PM and waited for the stage to arrive. It pulled in about 4:15. It was little more than a rough wagon with a few wooden seats built into it, covered by a canvas awning to keep the weather out. It was rough, but it sufficed. Wesley recognized the driver, John Fay.

Wesley walked up to the stage and caught John's eye. "John, long time!"

"Sherriff, how are you?"

"Fine, John. Did you drive the Sunday stage from Lee to Winsted?"

"No, Sherriff, that was Dave Merwin, the other driver. Why?"

"Want to know if he was flagged down in Cold Spring and picked up four colored men headed to Winsted Sunday morning."

"Not sure, Sherriff. You'll have to talk to Dave. He will be through here on my days off. Let's see," John pulled a tattered schedule from his pocket." Today's Tuesday… he'll be here Thursday, bout this time, northbound."

"Ok, I'll talk to him then. If I give you a letter for the Sherriff in Winsted, when could you get it there?"

"Headed in now, probably by eight tonight."

"Good. Let me write it out."

Wesley went into the Inn to borrow a pen and paper. He requested the Sherriff in Winsted detain the four colored men who had left Otis. He named them and requested that they be sent back to Otis to be questioned as soon as possible. He added a warning that a triple murder was involved, imploring the Connecticut Sherriff to use caution, and closed the note. He took the letter to the driver, pulled him aside, and told him his plan.

"John, these four colored men look like they might be suspects in a triple murder in Cold Spring. I need the law in Winsted to get them on the first stage north in the morning. I intend to arrest them, hold and question them until I get to the truth. Please tell them all this down in Winsted. How they work out the details is up to them. Tell them that I thank them in advance."

"OK, Sherriff. I'll tell 'em. Glad to help. Heard about that bad business."

"Thanks, John. See you tomorrow morning in Otis."

Wesley mounted up and spurred his horse north. Time to get help. He would stay in Otis tonight and send for Muncie. Things were moving fast.

Chapter Seven

Wednesday, September 10, 1862

Days Hotel, Otis Center

Otis, Massachusetts

8:00 AM

Wesley spent the night in Otis, renting a room at the Days Hotel. He had arrived the previous evening just before dusk. The first thing he did was locate a young man willing to ride to Monterey. He paid the lad to tell Sherriff Muncie that he needed him Wednesday morning in Otis before 7:00 AM.

The Days Hotel was a fixture in Otis. Located at the intersection of the Sandisfield-Lee Road and the road to Blandford, it commanded the major intersection in Otis. A plain building with a dining room downstairs and several rooms for rent on the second floor; it was simply decorated, more like an upscale farmhouse than a posh hotel. It had plaid red and white curtains and handmade bedspreads that lent a homey feel. In a word, it was comfortable.

The stage from Winsted wasn't due until 11:00 AM, so he had time to set things up. Wesley was up before dawn. He found a windowless room in the Town Hall to use as a holding room for the prisoners. It had a separate room down the hall so he could talk to them individually.

Muncie arrived at about 7:00 AM. Wesley immediately sent him to Lenox to pick up a jail wagon and brief the High Sherriff.

Wesley hoped Muncie would return before noon but doubted he could make the round trip in that amount of time. That left him to make the arrest alone, provide security for four prisoners, as well as question them. He recruited two men from the hotel restaurant and deputized them to help guard the prisoners for a few hours until Muncie got back from Lenox. He looked around and felt he was ready. He pulled out his pocket watch; it was only 8:30 AM.

Wesley was nervous; this was new territory for him. Questioning a murder suspect was way beyond what he had felt comfortable with just a few days ago. Now he felt it was within his grasp… maybe. He felt invested in this case, and that helped with the confidence factor. He realized he desperately wanted or maybe needed justice for this mother and her children. It gave him energy. This was a new and exciting feeling; he felt an almost reverent responsibility to the dead that he couldn't yet fathom.

He got breakfast at the hotel, and while he ate, he pondered his own feelings. So much of his life revolved around his past marriage; his late wife was the love of his life. She'd wanted children so badly, not for her, but to give to him. He had belatedly realized that he blamed himself for making her pregnant, maybe even causing her to die in childbirth. Was this… he searched for words, the obsession that was driving him to seek justice for this mother and her children? Was he just a grieving man? No, the voice in his head insisted, he was a Deputy Sherriff.

He had to put aside his personal struggle. He was the law, and the only justice the Jones family was likely to see. He felt strangely empowered and the most focused he had been since he buried his family. He was ready!

The stage pulled in at about 11:05. Wesley could see that the only passengers were the four colored half-brothers seated under the awning. At first glance, they looked sullen and resigned, but as Wesley watched, he noted sidelong glances in his direction that dripped cynicism and hatred.

Wesley walked up to the stage and noted the Sherriff in Winsted had wrapped up his prisoners like a Christmas present. They not only had wrist irons on but were chained by the ankles to the stage body.

Wesley looked at them, attempting to make eye contact. The four of them, in unison, looked at the floor of the coach. "You men, the four of you are under arrest for suspicion of murder. We're gonna have a long talk together. Now get down and follow my two deputies inside."

The four men looked around, and one of the Dolphin brothers said, "Don't know you, but you act like every other lawman. Who are we supposed to have a kilt?"

"Don't you worry; I'll explain it all to you. For now, just do as you're told," ordered Wesley.

A small crowd had gathered to watch the proceedings. Wesley was in the process of having the crowd move on when John Fay, the stage driver, approached him.

"Sherriff," he said, pulling Wesley away from the crowd. "The Sherriff in Winsted gave me a message for you. Says if you end up letting these four go, he wants them back. He thinks he will have a case to arrest em for theft in a few days. Says murder trumps theft for now. By the way, here are the keys for the irons."

"Thanks, John. They give you any trouble?"

"Naw, just scared a couple of other passengers onto a later stage, hand and leg irons and all."

"You did a real good job, John. Now let's see if I can do mine."

The deputies got the four into the windowless room in the Town Hall and had them sit down on the floor. Wesley asked one of the deputies to get four sandwiches and coffee from the hotel to feed the prisoners. He returned a few minutes later with the food. Wesley watched the four men eat. He pulled the deputies aside and told them that once he started talking to one of them, there would be no conversation between the rest of them until he finished talking to them all.

As Wesley watched the four, it became obvious that the two Dolphin brothers were close, sitting next to each other with much whispering between the two of them. Willis White sat alone but had a hard stare like he knew what was coming next. He probably had been through this before. Nelson Warner, the last of the four, looked to be the youngest of the bunch. He sat in a corner alone, looking scared and vulnerable. That's, Wesley thought, where he would start.

He waved one of his deputies over and whispered that he should bring Warner down to be interviewed alone after the prisoners finished eating.

Wesley went down to the interview room and waited. Earlier in the morning, he'd set the room up. He had emptied it out except for a small rough table and two chairs, one on each side of the table facing each other. He didn't want any unnecessary distractions for the prisoners. Wesley felt it was critical that he had their complete attention and controlled the conversation. It wasn't long before the door opened, and Warner shuffled in.

"Sit," ordered Wesley indicating the chair on the opposite side of the table from him.

Wesley said nothing else but observed the dark-skinned black man closely for several minutes. He was dressed in what looked like 3rd or 4th hand-me-down, patched clothes. They were dirty, and the man, well, there was no other way to say it, stunk. His body odor was overpowering. He seemed very nervous and never made eye contact with Wesley; he just stared at the floor. Wesley noted all of this and thought that this man had little self-esteem. That's the key, thought Wesley; this he could use.

They had been sitting silently for a few minutes when Wesley got up and took the key to the irons out of his pocket. Warner started at the noise of Wesley moving towards him, cowering back and down in the chair as if he was about to be beaten.

Wesley stopped. "Whoa, buddy," holding out the key. "Just want to give you a break from the irons. Hold out your legs and wrists." Wesley took the irons off gently. "There you go, you OK?"

"How can I be OK? You are accusing me of killing someone. I ain't killed nobody, ever! I've been black my whole life. I know how this works. Nobody ever believes what I say, and the law accuses me of any crime they can't pin on anyone else. Justice for a black man is just the white man's wish."

Wesley thought for a moment, then replied, "You will find I'm not like that at all. I'm color-blind. I'm only after the truth, that's all. I'll be honest with you if you're honest with me."

"I heard that line ten times; it was just before the cell door slammed each time."

"Tell me, how old are you?"

"I'll be 18 in a few months."

"You've been arrested before?"

"I told you. I'm black; therefore, the answer is yes," replied Warner.

"What for?"

"People always say I'm stealing their stuff."

"Do you?"

Warner shrugged, then looked up at Wesley and smiled.

"OK. Let's talk about last week. You worked at the Cold Spring Iron Works?"

"Yeah, me and my three half-brothers," he indicated with a wave toward where the others were being held. "We got a message from my dad, Thomas, that they needed extra help. We'd done that before, a couple of times. When we come up here, we stay the week with Thomas, his wife, and son James."

"When did you leave?"

"We caught the stage Sunday morning. Walked to the road and flagged it down about 8:00 AM or so."

Wesley thought for a moment. "You all left and stayed together the whole day Sunday?"

"Yup, till we got to Winsted."

"Tell me about your father and his family."

Warner looked up quizzically, "My Dad? Why?"

"Cause I want to know."

"Look, my dad may not be the best man in the world. He slept with so many women, white, black, and Spanish. He was just… in his messed-up mind, every woman's man. He bragged that some of them he had forced himself on. That's why I have so many half-brothers. You gotta understand Sherriff, a black man, especially in these parts, has got few black women to love. He's gotta take whatever comes his way, any way he can. My dad preaches that to all of us all the time. This white woman who finally shamed him into marrying her was the first who talked sense into him, and for her trouble, she gets beat when he's drunk, which is almost every day. Even so, he still brags to us boys that he gets sex with whoever, whenever and however he wants it. You know, Sherriff, the three of them live in that shack, if you can call it liven, and they know it won't get any better being a black man with a white woman. He knows it and lives with that every day. It's the lot of a black man, even worse for him with a white wife. So, if he takes liberties with the law, it evens out when the law takes liberties with them all."

"What about their son… what's his name?"

"James. He worships the old man. He is following in his father's footsteps. He doesn't know who he is yet; he is way too young. His father knows that and uses it to get him to do what he wants. James is the guy who fetches food for the family when Dad says he's hungry. The Sunday we left, they were going to meet that morning to kill a sheep James had stole and hid in the woods because Dad said he was hungry. Before you ask, I don't know who he took it from. Dad says jump. James asks how high?"

"What does James look like? How old is he?"

"He's 21 or 22, I think, but don't look it. He looks more my age. He's really light-skinned cause of his ma. That's about it."

"Nelson, I want you to think carefully before you answer this. Did your Dad or James talk about a white family, maybe a white neighbor that was always accusing them of stealing or milking their cow at night?

"They talked about some white lady like that, and they called her the 'bitch'. Said she did accuse them of that stuff, as you said. They didn't like her much, especially Dad. He didn't cotton to any woman who sassed him. James seemed to take it more in stride. His attitude was, oh well, she done caught me, so what? She ain't gonna do nothin' about it. They talked about her some but not all the time. Other than that, I don't know much."

"Ok Nelson, what are the others gonna tell me? That you lied to me?"

Warner laughed, "They ain't gonna say nothing. See, I'm the guy who got just a little of white man's justice. Them three, they spent more than half their lives livin' white man's justice; in Jail."

Wesley just stared at Warner, then opened the door and had the deputy return him to the other three. True to Warner's prediction, the other three were paraded one by one through the interrogation room without saying a single word. Wesley had run out of options.

About that time, Muncie rolled in with the jail wagon. He jumped down and approached Wesley. "The High Sherriff said to tell you that you did a good job."

Wesley shook his head, "I don't think they did it. I still got to hold 'em till I talk to the relief stage driver tomorrow. His word will make or break this. Can you bring 'em up to Lennox? Then meet me here tomorrow morning so I can update you. I'll buy breakfast."

"You got it, Wesley. Glad to help any way I can."

They loaded up the four colored men in the jail wagon, and Muncie headed north to Lennox and the county jail.

Chapter Eight

Thursday, September 11, 1862

Days Hotel, Otis Center

Otis, Massachusetts

7:30 AM

Wesley had again stayed at the Days Hotel in Otis the previous night. Dave Muncie had arrived to meet him at about 7:30 AM. They commandeered a table in the corner of the hotel dining room, drinking coffee while awaiting their breakfast. The dining room was simply decorated and more like someone's home than a hotel. There were red and white, gingham patterned, country-type curtains on the windows, and this was complemented by matching table clothes on the tables. The coffee was rich and hot, and the waitress nsured it was topped off fresh in the cups. The atmosphere was relaxed and pleasant.

Wesley brought Dave Muncie up to date. He told him about George Jones, the conversations with the doctors, and his interviews with the four black men the day before. Muncie listened intently.

Muncie was on the old side for a lawman pushing sixty. He was in great shape, tall, well over six feet, but barely two hundred pounds. His hair had thinned until he was on the verge of baldness. It gave him an air of knowledge. Despite this, he carried himself more like a 20-year-old. Wesley had always been impressed by his intellect and common sense.

After hearing all the details, Muncie suggested that he could meet the stage that day and talk to Dave Merwin, the relief driver, to check the story of the four black half-brothers. Wesley quickly agreed. He felt that the story would hold up, and he told Muncie this. They just didn't strike him as doing this. Muncie agreed with him, noting that he didn't yet have a feel for the case and counseling Wesley to wait and see where the facts took him. Wesley saw the wisdom in this advice and reluctantly agreed. Still, he had a feeling.

Maybe it was his gut talking, but everything was pointing to the black family with the white wife and mother, the Callanders. Wesley really didn't have any hard evidence other than a possible motive, the retaliation for the accusations made by Mrs. Jones. The sighting of the young light-skinned black man, by all accounts a good description of James by the fisherman, made it seem more plausible. The fact that the Callanders lived in and knew the immediate area and had admittedly stolen stock from local farms added more creditability yet. Finally, James had been caught one recent night milking Jones' cow less than a few hundred yards from the murder site. They were beginning to look like good suspects. He wanted to interview Thomas Callander and his son James as soon as possible.

Wesley and Muncie finished breakfast at about 9:00 AM and headed in separate directions, agreeing to meet back at the hotel the following morning to compare notes. Wesley mounted up and turned south, headed for the Cold Springs Iron Works and the Callanders. On the way out of town, he passed Dr. Spellman's place just as the County Coroner, Dr. Parsons, was parking his rig. He waved Wesley down.

As Wesley pulled up his horse, Parsons walked to meet him. "Sherriff, how goes it? I understand we have an arrest."

"Well doc, we do, but I talked with them, not that they said much, but I don't think they did it. I'll know more after the stage comes in later this afternoon."

"In light of that information, I am going to convene a coroner's inquest here in town. You, of course, will be a key witness. Give me a day to set it up, and you can plan on testifying on Monday afternoon. I will get word to you where we will hold the hearings."

Wesley sighed loudly, "Doc, I have work to do here, I feel I'm close, but I have to strike while the iron is hot."

"Sorry Sherriff, it's the law in unsolved homicide cases."

"OK, I'm on a pretty good hunch now, so let me go. Send someone to find me tomorrow to tell me when and where you'll need me."

"You got it, Sherriff. Good luck."

Wesley started down the road towards Cold Spring. As he rode along the river, he took a deep breath. The air was beginning to smell like fall. The moisture from the river combined with the smell of the decaying leaves was occasionally intermixed with the smell of hay or manure as he passed the scattered farms. It was so…. well…Berkshire. He realized he probably wouldn't want to live anywhere else. He passed the Jones's farm and saw George out doing chores. It was good to see him moving around.

Minutes later, he pulled up in front of the Cold Springs Iron Works office. It was almost 10:30 AM. The air smelled of coal smoke and sulfur, and there were raw iron ingots scattered about, many with rust streaks down their side. The office was a simple shack with a desk inside. Wesley entered and found a man he assumed ran the foundry seated inside.

"Hello, Henry Mellis," Wesley said, reading the name from a dirty nameplate on the desk. "I'm Sherriff Wesley Langdon. I was investigating the murder of the Jones family last weekend, just a few farms north of here. I'm interested in talking to two fellows who work for you, James and Thomas Callander."

"Sherriff, those boys work for me all day. I count on them to keep my furnace hot. Once the correct temperature is reached first thing in the morning, they can't stop, or else the furnace cools, and the run of iron stops. Then we got to start all over. Costs a good deal of money if that happens.

I'm asking you to wait till the end of the day to do your talking. We started cooling the furnace 'bout 3:00. Those boys were done hauling coal then, just cleaning up. That would be a better time. Look, I know you have a job to do, but so do I. Can we work something out here?"

Wesley pulled out his watch and saw it was only 10:30, so he would have to return in four and a half hours. "Tell you what, you have those two here waiting for me at 3:30 PM, and I'll let you have your day."

"Thanks. Look, one good turn deserves another. Listen, I know it's none of my business Sherriff, and I don't know what you want to talk to them about, but I can tell you they've been workin' for me on and off for about a year now. They're lazy as a big fat sow hog, and you got to stay on 'em to keep 'em in line, but I've come to know them pretty well. I can tell you the father has a big chip on his shoulder concerning white men. I doubt you're gonna get him to talk at all, an' if he's sitting with his kid, the kid won't talk to you either. Don't want to tell you how to do your job, but if I was you, I'd talk to the kid alone. He's young, and without his dad, he is lost in the real world you and I live in. Just sayin.'"

Wesley thought for a second. "Henry, you know these two much better than I do, so I trust your judgement. Better than talking to them without knowing things like this. Ok, here's what we're gonna do, get the kid here at three-thirty.

Can you distract the old man? Maybe have him doing something away from the office, out of sight from here?

"Number three furnace is down and needs to be cleaned; I can have him do that. It will take him all afternoon. He won't know you're here until after you're done with the kid. What are you after from the kid anyway?"

"Just want to see what he has to say about the family that was killed."

"You think he had something to do with it?"

"Time will tell. See you around three, and much obliged for the advice."

Mellis just nodded.

Wesley now had time on his hands. He headed back to the doctors to discuss the coroner's inquest. His horse responded to the fresh late summer coolness, and he had to rein it in several times. He did his best thinking on the back of a horse. The soothing rhythmic motion of the animal lent itself to physical relaxation, allowing the mind to wander. Wesley wondered if he was close to solving the case or if this was just another dead end. He knew from his reading that most crimes should be solved quickly; those that weren't often remained unsolved forever.

He decided he'd jumped the gun on the four half-brothers from Winsted and vowed not to rush to judgement in the future. He was deep in thought and almost rode by the doctor's residence before he realized his error. He quickly reined in the horse, pulling up to the hitching post.

Wesley knocked on the doctor's door and entered to find Spellman and Parsons sitting at the kitchen table, deep in conversation. The three greeted each other warmly, a trait Wesley noted that seemed to come from the feeling that they were together in this…. crusade for justice. Wesley told the doctors of his conversation with the owner of the Iron Works and his plans to return that afternoon.

Parsons interrupted Wesley, "Sherriff, from what you're telling me, you can put this colored boy in the area about the time this happened. You have documented an ongoing problem between that black family and the Jones woman, and you know they have been to the Jones farm stealing things. Sounds to me like you have motive and opportunity. Now if you can only put the murder weapons in this boy's hands, you will have solved this thing."

"Doc, just how do I do that?"

Spellman broke in, "Maybe you don't have to. The Jones woman had torn and broken fingernails on both hands and debris that looked like human tissue under what was left. Maybe she got her hands on her attacker. There could be scratches or other wounds on this boy's body. That would help put him there when she was killed."

Wesley pondered on this for a moment, "Something else to look for, I suppose. I think I made a mistake rushing to arrest those four from Winsted. I won't make that mistake again. I want to take my time and be thorough. My intention is to play possum with the boy and his family, not let them think I'm on to 'em. That way, they won't rabbit on me." Changing the subject, Wesley added, "I hope you two will stay close. These conversations help to sort things out."

Parsons and Spellman, in tandem, nodded. "As long as you need us, Sherriff, we'll be here."

Parsons added, "I'll convene the coroner's inquest Monday morning. Sitting a jury will take most of the morning, so figure out testifying right after lunch. If I were you and I'm the one asking the questions, I would stick to what you saw at the scene and avoid directing suspicion towards anyone. That will help you with your plan on watching the Callanders."

Wesley nodded. "Thanks doc; I never had to do an inquest before, so that's good advice. How long do you expect to keep me?"

"Oh, I believe we can finish up with you in the afternoon. Don't want to keep you from your work any longer than we have to. If I were you, I would consider your interview this afternoon. Given what you've told us, there are some strategies you can employ. Separating him from his father is a good start, but you're gonna need to play on his insecurity of not having his father there with him. Don't be gentle; you must make him answer your questions right then and there without his dad.”

Spellman admonished, “Take a good look at his face, neck, and arms. Based on my past observations, that’s where women mostly leave scratches or bite marks during attacks. You might get lucky. Make him explain those wounds and how he got them. I have faith in you, Sherriff; you have a good head on your shoulders. We’re here for you.”

With that, Wesley wished the doctors well and mounted up. It was now almost 1:00 PM. He could get to the Iron Works in about half an hour, so he had time to burn. He headed back to the Day’s Hotel in Otis to grab lunch and plan his interview with James Callandar.

Chapter Nine

Thursday, September 11, 1862

Cold Springs Iron Works

Otis, Massachusetts

3:10 PM

Wesley rode up to the Iron Works just after 3:00 PM and was ushered into an empty room in the back of the office that held only a table and a few chairs. The owner then went to fetch James Callendar. Wesley used these few minutes to clear all the chairs from around the table except for two. He positioned one on each side of the table, so they faced each other across the table. Satisfied, he waited. It wasn't long before he heard the owner coming with someone else.

The door opened, and a tall, thin, very light-skinned, young-looking, colored boy of about 20 was ushered into the room. His patched wool clothes were soaked with sweat and covered with black coal dust. At first glance, he looked like an innocent teenager. He was obviously tired, and his face was streaked with sweat that ran through the coal dust caking his face, giving the impression he was constantly crying. His eyes were at half-mast from fatigue. Wesley thanked, then excused Mr. Mellis, the owner, and introduced himself to James as the Sherriff investigating the Jones murder. The mention of the murder brought an instant response from James. His eyes went from half shut to wide open, and he franticly looked about the room. Wesley noted this and asked James to be seated. Reluctantly James complied. Wesley took a seat across the table from him.

Wesley didn't say anything else but just looked at the boy up and down. He noted an irritated-looking red scratch that ran from just under James' left ear down his cheek circling around and ending just short of his chin. It was red and angry looking, very evident through the coal dust, and looked bad enough to have bled when it was inflicted. He noted a much less severe scratch an inch or so below the bigger scratch as it ran across the cheek. It ran parallel, more or less, to the more severe scratch. Both injuries looked a few days old but appeared to have been inflicted at the same time. Wesley let the silence hang. The boy would not lock eyes with him.

Finally, Wesley sighed and said, "Son, we need to talk. I want you to know that I have found out a lot about you."

At this, Wesley could have sworn the boy's eyes grew wider if that was possible.

Wesley continued, "James, I know you were in the area of the Jones's farm last Sunday morning. That's when Mrs. Jones and her two kids were murdered. I also know you were stealing from the Jones farm and that Mrs. Jones caught you one-night last week. Anything else you want to tell me?"

James just stared arrogantly back at him.

"Ok, let's try this one on for size. Early that Sunday morning, you used a boat that didn't belong to you up on Cotton Pond. Right after that, you left the pond to meet your dad to butcher a stolen lamb in the woods right near the Jones farm. How am I doing, James?"

James looked at Wesley, but the look in his eyes had changed. Instead of an arrogant, hateful stare, they were now full of fear.

Finally, James spoke, "Sherriff, I don't know what you think I did. If you had proof, you'd be arresting me. I live just down the road. I'm always out in the woods looking for food. You gonna arrest me or not, cause if you're not, I'm leavin'."

Wesley interrupted, "What I can't understand is why kill the little kids?"

"I didn't kill no kids." James almost spat out the reply. It was the sincerest thing Wesley thought he had said.

"Only one more question. That scratch on your cheek, how did you get it?"

"Got that berry pickin' the other day down Sandisfield way. Now I'm leaving."

With that, he walked out the door. Wesley watched him go, but secretly he smiled to himself. Now he felt he was right; James was involved in the murder. James' responses were about what he expected, but his body language suggested someone was lying. He felt James's response to not killing the children was sincere. That reinforced the doctor's theory that there was a second person. Who was the second person?

As if on cue, the door burst open, and a large, powerfully built colored man filled the frame. "Sherriff, you listen; you want to talk to any my kin, you come to see me first. You hear me! Are you trying to pin something on my boy? Always blame the colored man; I know your game. Ain't gonna happen this time. You hear me." After he was finished, he stood at the door breathing hard, his eyes ablaze with hatred.

Wesley sized Thomas Callandar up. He was black with a very dark complexion, over six feet tall, and well-muscled from his work. Wesley thought he would not want to get this guy mad. He had coal dust staining his face with ample perspiration drawing lines in the dust as it ran down his face. He seemed intense, set in his ways and thoughts, and just … formidable.

Wesley walked up to him and quietly said, "Just who the hell are you?"

"My name is Thomas Callendar, and I'll tell you who you can talk to…"

Wesley interrupted him and, in a quiet voice, said, "This says I can talk to whoever, whenever, and however I want, "as he held out his badge in the palm of his left hand. With

76

his right hand, he pointed his index finger in Callendar's face and finished his remark. "I believe that's what you tell your boys about raping any woman you want."

Callendar's face blanched, and his mouth fell open. He backed out of the doorway without saying another word.

Wesley knew he had accomplished a lot. They now knew they had to watch their step. Yet they still were not sure how much more Wesley knew. Confusion in their minds would only help his cause. He exited the room, thanked Henry Mellis, the foundry owner, and rode out towards Sandisfield and home.

Wesley thought as he rode toward home that he wasn't much of a cook. Many years ago, his mother had taught him the basics of cooking. She had stressed that if you threw the ingredients into a pot and then brought up the heat and allowed it to simmer for a good long while, you often got excellent results. Wesley thought that investigations were a lot like cooking. The ingredients were in the pot, and the pot was boiling. He felt he only had to be patient, let it simmer, and wait for everything to come together.

Chapter Ten

Friday, September 12, 1862

Days Hotel

Otis, Massachusetts

7:30 AM

Wesley had gotten up early, riding from his farm in Sandisfield to the Days Hotel in Otis to meet Sherriff Muncie. Wesley was already on his first cup of coffee when Muncie walked in. After greeting each other, they quickly got down to business. Muncie told Wesley that the story of the four black half-brothers of James Callender checked out with the stage driver. That meant they were on the stage, almost out of the state, when Emily Jones was killed. Muncie had already filed paperwork to release the four from custody. Wesley really wasn't surprised by this development.

Over a breakfast of delicious hotcakes drowned in maple syrup, Wesley briefed Muncie on his interview with James and the run-in with Thomas. Muncie agreed that there appeared to be more than just suspicion linking James to the murder. The scratch was of special interest to Muncie, and he urged Wesley to consult the doctors to see if there was any way to link it to the murder. He commented that it might be the first hard evidence they had uncovered. He also suggested, prefaced by a remark that the politicians had to be appeased, that they meet the following Tuesday morning with Berkshire District Attorney Gillett in Lenox. It was time to run all the information by him; that way, he could advise the Sheriffs on how he wanted to proceed. Wesley agreed and asked Muncie to set up the meeting.

The two then strategized testimony for the coroner's inquest the following Monday. They agreed that the best course of action was to simply describe the crime scene. If questioned further, they would reply that they were interviewing witnesses daily to get to the truth.

Wesley then suggested Muncie keep a quiet eye on the Callander place to make sure the family didn't just up and leave. Wesley felt he hadn't pressured the family too much in his interview but didn't want to take any chances. They didn't know Muncie, and he could fit into the surroundings without arousing suspicion. Muncie agreed this was a good precaution, and they decided that they would meet each night about dark, at the New Boston Inn in Sandisfield, out of the public eye, to compare notes. Hopefully, this would keep the surveillance quiet. With business out of the way, they finished breakfast and lingered over a third cup of coffee.

At about 9:30 AM, the two Sheriffs separated even though they were both headed south. They had both thought it was better for Muncie not to leave with Wesley. He would meander out of town on his own so he would not raise any suspicion on his way to the Callander place.

Wesley rode to Dr. Spellman's to get his opinion on the scratches he had seen on James' cheek. He was pleased to see Dr. Parsons' rig tied up out front when he arrived. After all, two opinions were better than one. Wesley walked into the office area to find the two doctors pouring over paperwork. They looked up and greeted him warmly.

Wesley told the doctors of his meeting the preceding day with James Callander, describing, in detail, the scratches on his neck.

Parsons listened intently, then asked, "How did he say he got the scratches?"

"Berry picking about a week before in Sandisfield."

Parsons scratched his chin, "doesn't make sense to me. The only berries left this time of year are the low-bush blackberries. They grow at most about a foot high. No way they're going to scratch a six-foot man on the cheek unless he's crawling on his belly."

Spellman added, "You describe the scratches as starting under his ear, coming around to the front of his face by his chin as if he turned his head or entire body while being scratched.

Wesley thought a moment, "Yes, and that doesn't happen much in any berry patch, least of all low bush blackberries."

Spellman continued, "The second parallel scratch sounds a lot like a second finger with less pressure. Is that what it looked like to you, Wesley?"

Wesley thought for a moment. "I never put that together, but yes, that's exactly what it looked like."

Parsons summed up what all three were thinking: "We are all convinced this was done by the Jones woman during the attack, but it's all just speculation, educated speculation, but still not the proof we need."

Wesley just nodded. He was at a dead end. Now it was up to the District Attorney to make a call. Did they have enough information to arrest James Callander? Patience … deep breaths, Wesley cautioned himself. Let those that have to prosecute the case make those weighty decisions. Meanwhile, keep gathering facts and evidence; that was his job.

Chapter Eleven

Tuesday, September 16, 1862

Berkshire District Attorney's Office

Main Street

Lennox, Massachusetts

1:30 PM

Wesley and Sherriff Muncie were seated in the waiting room of the District Attorney for Berkshire County, the Honorable Ward B. Gillett. They had left Otis after meeting there at 7:30 that morning. The ride to Lennox had taken two and a half hours. They passed those hours discussing all that had happened since they had last met on Sunday night at the Inn in Sandisfield. The Callanders had shown no signs of leaving, to the relief of both men. Neither Sherriff wanted to be put in the situation of arresting the family without judicial approval for what would be no doubt a capital crime.

Both had been present at the Coroner's inquest in Otis the preceding day. Six, very bored citizens, dozed while the particulars of the case were presented before them. Wesley doubted they would come to any useful conclusions. Nevertheless, he did his duty, recounting the crime scene in detail and summarizing the husband's alibi and his investigation upholding it. It seemed a waste of time and effort.

The two sheriffs were on the verge of dozing when the District Attorney came out of his office to greet them. Wesley's first impression was a "stuffed shirt." He was impeccably dressed in a suitcoat and tie with ruffles about his neck, ready, Wesley thought, for a Presidential Inauguration.

He obviously was well fed and reminded Wesley of a spring pig, fattened up for slaughter, with his short legs and rotund belly. His hair, what little was left, was greying. All in all, his appearance suggested a man with an inflated sense of himself. That, thought Wesley, left one with some doubt of the veracity of his word. Introductions were made, and they were shown into the man's well-appointed office.

The office seemed to support Wesley's first impression of the man. The desk was huge and highly polished walnut, Wesley guessed. The walls were adorned with degrees and diplomas interspersed with letters signed by both state and national dignitaries. Clearly, the intent was to make one feel they were in the presence of greatness. Wesley wasn't impressed; he had heard all too often about politicians who were not to be trusted in offices such as this. Wesley had to stop and take a moment to compose himself, remembering that they needed the man's help.

Once they were comfortably seated, the District Attorney began. "Gentlemen, I have heard from both High Sherriff Root and the Governor regarding this case. Both feel this case has ramifications well beyond the small hamlet where it occurred. There are considerations, politically, that must be weighed here. But enough of that; that's my worry. Yours is to find out who did this reprehensible deed. What have you learned?"

Wesley looked at Muncie, who nodded, indicating Wesley should start. Wesley described in detail the crime scene, the doctor's medical examination, and conclusions, including the fact that more than one assailant was more than likely present during the murder.

He detailed his investigation into the husband and the witness who saw the young, light-skinned black man in the area at the time of the crime.

Wesley discussed in detail the thieving of James Callander at many farms in the area. He emphasized the episode at the Jones place where he got caught by Mrs. Jones only a few days before the murder. That, coupled with what James' half-brother had told him about their calling her the 'bitch', suggested this as motivation for the murder. Muncie occasionally interrupted to drive home details in the timeline and other important facts they wanted to highlight. Wesley thought they were making a good team.

Wesley took his time with his background investigation into the Callenders, omitting no details. He wanted to paint the picture as he saw it. He spent a lot of time repeating what the iron works' owner told him, using it to tie the father and son's actions together. He used that to put into perspective the other information he obtained in his interview with the half-brother from Winsted. He finished with his interview with James Callender, emphasizing the fact that the only statement he did utter was that he didn't kill the kids. Wesley drove home his interpretation of this answer and the likelihood that the father and son had committed the crime together.

He described in detail the scratches on James' cheek, his excuse for the scratch, and the unlikelihood he could have gotten it in that way. He added the doctor's hypothesis of the parallel scratches being made by adjoining fingers. When Wesley finished, he looked up at the clock and was amazed that an hour and fifteen minutes had passed. The District Attorney sat with his hands folded, holding his chin upon them the whole time.

Several minutes of silence passed after Wesley finished, and they could see the District Attorney was weighing his thoughts and words carefully.

Finally, the hands dropped to the desk. "Gentlemen, you have done a fine job with very little evidence to go on. I admire your tenacity and will pass that on to Sherriff Root. That being said, there is not much more than a circumstantial case here.

Solid, but still circumstantial. You must remember the political realities here: our Governor is a diehard abolitionist.

If we were to prosecute a free, colored man and it appeared to be a witch hunt, it might undermine the support for his abolitionist stance among those with the monetary means to finance such a stance. I believe our dear Governor has eyes for higher office, probably in Washington. He will be very sensitive to any criticism this matter might bring from his financial supporters or his political opponents. Events to which you might or might not be privy on the national level further reduce our political leverage in this case. All that being said, a woman and two children were murdered, and I believe you have identified the culprits. With all of this to consider, I believe I need more time to navigate the politics and weigh the facts and circumstances you have so professionally presented today before I make any decision. I promise you that before the month is over, you will have that decision. Now if you don't mind, I am due in court."

Wesley could hardly contain his disappointment and was about to comment further on his distain of the intricacies of political involvement in the judicial system when Muncie grabbed his arm and led him out of the office. Once outside, Wesley started to go on about stuffed shirt politicians, but Muncie stopped him short. "Look, Wesley, like it or not, this is the guy that makes these decisions. You and I, we try and pursue justice based on what really happened. The people here have to factor in a lot of other things, chief among them, if they can convict this guy. He listened and, I think, approved of our facts and conclusions, give him a chance to work his political magic. I got a good feeling about this."

Wesley sighed, "I hope you are right. This is enough to make me give up this job."

"Wesley, you're being forced to merge the truth with politics. You are playing with the big boys now; you might never be again. Understand, learn, and you'll be a better Sherriff for it. Trust me on this; he is an ally, not an enemy. That's why I suggested we do it this way. Just give him a chance."

They mounted up and headed south to Otis. Little did they know that unimaginable events were about to unfold in Maryland and Washington, D.C., that would influence both the political atmosphere and public opinion involved with this case.

The first event, the Battle of Antietam in Sharpsburg, Maryland, occurred on September 17th, 1862, the single bloodiest day of warfare in United States history. Even more important to western Massachusetts public opinion, twenty-one regiments of Massachusetts troops were in the thick of battle and represented many of the unions' 12,400 killed and 9,550 wounded. The lists of the dead and wounded dominated local newspapers and cast a sad pall across the lives of the Berkshire citizenry for weeks.

The second event was the issuing of the Preliminary Emancipation Proclamation by President Lincoln on

September 22, 1862. This freed all slaves held in Confederate states as of January 1, 1863. It effectively changed public opinion regarding the reason for the war away from the country's reunification, refocusing it instead on freeing the colored man from slavery.

The latter wasn't as popular as the first. Discussion in the U.S. Congress, widely reported in the press, began to debate the constitutional status of a free colored man and how this would affect the country's society.

In response, local Berkshire papers wrote highlighted articles that debated how whites and blacks were different or the same. Some articles began asking whether this new cause was worth fighting for considering the large number of local casualties just in from Antietam. The debate was rehashed in Granges, watering holes, and church gatherings throughout the county.

In the midst of these events on the national stage, the Otis Selectmen voted to post a $500.00 reward, a large sum of money, given the economic severity of the war debt, for information leading to an arrest and conviction in the Jones murder case.

Wesley stayed abreast of these events, often wondering how or if they would play into the political winds blowing across his investigation. He would soon find out.

Chapter Twelve

Monday, September 22, 1862

Dining Room, Days Hotel

Otis, Massachusetts

Noon

Strange things were happening. Wesley and Muncie had been summoned to the Days Hotel dining room to meet a delegate sent by District Attorney Gillet. In a message delivered the day before, they were told to meet at noon and assist the gentlemen as necessary.

A few minutes after noon, two well-dressed men entered the room. Muncie recognized one of the men and greeted him warmly. He introduced him to Wesley as Officer John Day from the staff of the State Supreme Court. He explained that they had worked together on several cases in the past.

Day introduced the second man. "Sheriffs, this is the Honorable Judge Dewey of the Massachusetts Supreme Court. He has been tasked with examining James Callander at the request of District Attorney Gillett to ascertain facts relevant to the Jones family murder."

Wesley looked at Muncie, who shrugged and said, "I've never heard of such a procedure before, but I trust Gillett. What do you need?"

Day asked, "How soon can you have James Callander here?"

Wesley replied, "I can get him here in an hour and a half. What if he won't come?"

Day explained he was in possession of a summons requiring him to appear and would accompany Wesley to pick up the man. He asked Muncie to procure a room or office where the judge might examine Callander. Officer Day was obviously used to being in charge. Although it rankled Wesley that he appeared to be taking over the investigation, there was obvious planning behind it.

Day addressed Wesley: "I'm saddled up; the sooner we leave, the better I like it."

Wesley asked Muncie to borrow his horse, Callander would not have one of his own to ride.

The two men mounted up with Muncie's horse in tow and quietly rode south toward the foundry.

Once out of town, Wesley could stand it no more. "John, what the hell is going on?"

Day laughed, "Wow, you held your tongue longer than I would have." Turning serious, he continued. "It's all good. Gillett feels the more varied opinions we have concluding this James Callander is guilty, the more insulated certain politicians will be. I believe you are well on your way to an arrest warrant, but let's let that be our secret."

Wesley just shook his head. "Never thought I would be involved with politics in this job."

"That's just it," explained Day, "This will insulate you and Muncie as the investigating officers from a defense charge that the arrest was politically motivated."

"Is it?"

Day thought a moment before answering. "When there is a chance that a man's life hangs in the balance within the judicial system, politics play into the equation. Add the fact that this is a colored man who might be accused of raping and killing a white woman, and all bets are off. The President could not have chosen a worse time for his Emancipation Proclamation with respect to this case. With our governor's outspoken abolitionist stance in this state, the political climate for finding a colored man guilty is tenuous at best. Let's just concentrate on our job, proving he did it and getting a conviction."

They rounded the bend and saw the dark smoke of the furnaces at the foundry.

"We're almost there," Wesley said. "We can expect trouble from his father. He won't like this at all. For that matter, neither will the foundry owner."

"Wesley, you seem like you can handle yourself. I'll take care of James. You stay between us and the father. If he interferes, we arrest him. No discussion, no debate."

They were turning into the foundry when Wesley responded with a grin, "I think I'm going to like working with you, Day."

They entered the foundry and explained what was happening to Mr. Millett. He was not pleased. Nevertheless, he went out and got James from the factory grounds and brought him to the office. James wasn't happy to see Wesley again when he entered the office.

Officer Day explained what was going on. James wasn't under arrest; this was only a summons to appear to talk and that Wesley would see he got home after they were finished. James seemed to relax after the explanation. His father was nowhere to be seen, and they quickly rode off towards Otis.

There was little conversation on the ride back to the Days Hotel. Upon their arrival, Muncie was waiting for them. He indicated a room just off the dining room where the magistrate was waiting. Day took James in, indicating the two Sheriffs were to wait outside.

Muncie was full of questions, telling Wesley the Judge would say little about what was happening, but did not seem very happy to be there. Wesley related his conversation with Day, explaining what was going on. Muncie scratched his head, explaining this was something he had never heard of before.

Muncie then smiled. "Told you to trust Gillett. He figured out a way to get it done."

The two waited for almost an hour until the door swung open, and Day exited.

"Well," demanded Wesley, "What happened?"

Day pulled them into a quiet corner. "He didn't admit to anything. He got mad when we accused him of killing the Jones kids. He insisted he didn't kill the little kids but wouldn't say much else. He did start going back and changing parts of his story. I think he will eventually admit to everything, but not yet. Right now, I have to get the Judge back home to Lee, and you two need to get James back to work or home. At all costs, we need to avoid any insinuation later that we railroaded this guy. We need to show we upheld our end of the deal."

Wesley nodded, "What's next?"

"Depends on Gillett, but I bet you will hear from him before the week is out or early next week at the latest."

With that, they said farewell as the Judge and James entered the dining room. Wesley asked James where he wanted to be dropped off, and he indicated his home. They rode off to the south, again borrowing Muncie's horse. Wesley tried to initiate a conversation several times with James, who remained sullen and quiet. Wesley was back in Otis an hour later. Muncie was waiting for him.

"Did they tell you anything before they left?" Wesley asked.

"They were quiet as a church mouse, hardly said goodbye before they rode off."

"Suppose we'll just have to be patient. I'm headed home," Wesley declared. Wesley secretly doubted he could remain patient, but he had little choice. With the tip of his hat towards Muncie, he wheeled his horse around and headed south.

Chapter Thirteen

Saturday, September 27, 1862

Dining Room, Days Hotel

Otis, Massachusetts

9:00 AM

John Day was true to his word. Three days after the visit by Day and the magistrate, Wesley received a message. He was to get hold of Muncie and to wait at the Days Hotel in Otis Saturday morning, September 27th, at 9:30 AM. The message went on to say that Day had, in his hand, a signed arrest warrant for James Callender for three counts of Murder. They would serve the warrant together Saturday morning. Day admonished that secrecy must be observed until they had him in custody.

Wesley, understandably excited, had arrived at the Hotel at 7:30 AM Saturday morning. He had eaten breakfast but kept glancing at the clock. Time dragged. Muncie showed up just before 9:00 AM and joined Wesley. He had a good chuckle at Wesley's expense, watching him trying to drink coffee, hands shaking with excitement.

At 9:30 AM, John Day showed up alone and sat with them, ordering breakfast. Wesley was fit to be tied; he wanted to go.

Day calmed Wesley down. "Wesley, deep breaths. Been through this too many times; no need to rush. The jail wagon will meet us here at about noon, we have plenty of time. We need to do some planning before we go. We are going to the foundry. I understand they work until 1:00 PM on Saturdays. We know he will be there. Wesley, you and Muncie will take care of the father if he makes a scene.

I'll serve the warrant. I want to be in and out fast. That will minimize the chances of anything going wrong. Muncie will cuff him, and he will ride double on Muncie's horse in front of you; you've done this before. If the father becomes a problem, we arrest and cuff him to one of the iron ingots scattered in the foundry yard. Wesley, you will have to stay with him until I can get you help. Questions?"

Muncie and Wesley both shook their heads. It was very clear, and both approved of the plan.

Wesley asked, "What happens after the arrest?"

"We bring him here, meet the jail wagon, and turn him over to those officers, and they will bring him to the Lennox jail. He sits there till Monday when he gets arraigned, really just a legal formality. At the arraignment, they will set a bond. The Callanders can't raise that kind of money, so he will sit in jail until we are ready to bring the case to the Grand Jury."

Officer Day continued: "The three of us are scheduled to meet with the District Attorney in his office Monday morning at 10:00 AM. Plan on spending the day? It's time to start putting a case together for the Grand Jury and trial court. You think it's been hard up to this point? This was the easy part. Now we have to dot the I's and cross the T's. Boring, grueling leg work, identifying and prepping witnesses, real detective work. Believe me; the District Attorney is a stickler for detail and a tough taskmaster. Just remember, it's your case. You two have done a great job so far. Let's all work together to bring justice to the Jones family."

"How long before the Grand Jury meets?" Wesley asked.

"We have as long as it takes. There is no time limit to get an arrested prisoner before the Grand Jury. We do have to arraign him in court within three days so they can set a bond. Then he sits in jail until we are ready. The Grand Jury belongs to us. The District Attorney prosecutes or presents the case. There is no defense presented that is saved for court. So long as we can persuade the Grand Jury to pass a bill of inditement, the case goes to trial."

Officer Day finished his coffee with a gulp. "You lawmen ready to do your sworn duty?"

They nodded yes.

"Then let's go."

Wesley thought the ride to the foundry was tense. Little conversation passed between them. A million thoughts swirled through Wesley's mind; he worried he would make a mistake and mess the whole case up. He really felt like a greenhorn or a kid on his first real adventure, but this was serious work. Strangely, he thought of his late wife, and it was as if she was there with him. Inexplicitly, it calmed him down. Then they were around the bend from the foundry.

Day reined them to a stop. "Remember, professional, confident demeanor. We are in charge. That will go a long way to preventing trouble. We all know the plan. Let's get it done."

They rode into the foundry yard three abreast. Wesley imagined they presented a formidable front. The foundry owner was out in front of the office talking with both James and his father, Thomas. They reined up, dismounted, and walked over to the trio. Officer Day held out his badge and introduced the three of them.

"James Callender, I have a warrant for your arrest for three counts of Murder. You are under arrest."

Muncie immediately moved towards James. Thomas started to step between the two, blocking Muncie.

Wesley cautioned: "Wouldn't do that if I were you. It would be tough on the wife if both her men were thrown in jail."

Wesley started to move towards Thomas, but Day put a handout, stopping him.

"Mr. Callander, he's right. This is going to happen either way. Why make it worse?"

Thomas Callander stared at the three of them. There was hatred in his eyes. Wesley mentally braced himself for a physical confrontation.

Thomas continued his stare, but his body language relaxed. "You listen to me, boy," addressing James, who had by this time been handcuffed and was being led to Muncie's horse. "You don't say nothin'. These lawmen," he said, spitting out the word lawmen, "they mean to twist anything you say to make you look guilty. Say nothin! You understand me, boy?"

James simply nodded as Muncie pushed him into the saddle and climbed behind him. Wesley and John Day tipped their hats to the foundry owner, backed out, mounted up, and the three horses and four men rode north.

They were about halfway back to Otis Center when James spoke up. "What's gonna happen to me?"

Officer Day answered him. "James, you're going to be held at the Lennox Jail, arraigned on Monday morning, where bond will be set. Before we get to Otis and put you in the jail wagon, is there anything you want to say? Now is a good time to help yourself."

James looked at him and said, "I didn't kill those kids. That's all I'll say."

The rest of the ride passed in silence. The jail wagon was waiting when they arrived in Otis. Wesley involuntarily jumped when the iron door slammed shut after James had been thrust inside. He momentarily wondered what James must be thinking, locked up like an animal. A small, silent crowd witnessed the transfer to the jail wagon, including Rev. Thomas Hall.

Once the transfer to the jail wagon was done, the wagon left immediately for Lennox, accompanied by Officer Day. Muncie and Wesley had a short conversation agreeing to meet Monday morning at 7:00 AM at Day's Hotel for the ride to Lennox. Muncie then turned towards home. Wesley noted that Rev. Hall closely watched the goings on.

Once Muncie was out of sight, the Reverend approached Wesley. "Did you arrest him for the Jones murder?"

"Can't talk about the case Reverend, but yes, we had an arrest warrant for James Callander for the Jones family murder."

"Wish I could talk to that child, make him understand what he's done. I'd tell him the truth would set him free."

"Well, Reverend, I'm sure they would welcome you volunteering your time to save the souls of those poor boys in the Lennox jail. Right now, I've got work to do. Goodbye."

Wesley mounted up and was about to spur his horse southward when Reverend Hall spoke up. "Sherriff, I know you don't approve of my unfettered dedication to my flock. I suppose that it appears to be contrary to those personal human struggles we all face. Some tell me it makes me seem aloof, but I am human, you know." Surprisingly he chuckled. "Sherriff, you have done your job very well. Thank you." With that, he turned and walked towards the parsonage.

Wesley shook his head and smiled. He thought that despite his tough outer shell, there was a real person under that clerical collar. Maybe he would volunteer at the jail in Lennox. Certainly, they would welcome his help. With that, he wheeled his horse south and took some time off to clear his head. Little could Wesley know how prophetic his thoughts would become.

Chapter Fourteen

Monday, September 29, 1862

Berkshire County District Attorney's Office

Lennox, Massachusetts

10:00 AM

Officer Day met Muncie and Wesley in the Berkshire County District Attorney's waiting room. Within minutes they were ushered into the District Attorney's office. Mr. Gillett's office was much different than the previous visit. There were papers spread out across his massive desk, and he was moving rapidly around the mess. He wore no coat, and his shirtsleeves were rolled up above the elbows. He was talking to himself, more precisely carrying on an animated conversation with himself. He glanced in their direction as they entered, but that was as much initial acknowledgment as they got.

Finally, after several minutes, he spun around and immediately launched into a monologue aimed at the three lawmen. "There are a lot of loose ends to tie up before we convene a Grand Jury. Luckily, I have more than enough probable cause for the arraignment at 2:00 PM today, thanks to the job you two Sheriffs did. Good thing there are three of you to follow up on all these leads."

He then explained that they needed to identify and prepare witnesses that saw James Callander on the morning of the murder and could place him near, or better yet, at the Jones farm. This led to a discussion on how to go about all of that.

Wesley's local knowledge was invaluable in coming up with a list of people to talk to. They agreed that John Day would remain in Lennox to take care of issues that came up there while Muncie and Wesley would work on interviewing and identifying potential witnesses back in Otis. They were reviewing the timeline from the day of the murder when a secretary entered and announced that it was 1:30 and they were due in court in half an hour. Gillett excused himself to get ready, and Officer Day led Wesley and Muncie toward the County Courthouse, which was on the town green just around the corner from the District Attorney's office.

Wesley saw the building as they rounded the corner. It was a granite building built in the Greek Revival style of most northeastern government buildings. The granite was stained black in areas belying the buildings' age. Despite this, it was one of the most impressive buildings Wesley had ever seen. It dominated the town green and exuded the authority that emanated from the proceedings held within. They entered through the massive wooden front doors, which had to be at least ten feet high, and Day inquired at an information desk which of the four courtrooms the arraignment would take place in. Day led them in as they entered the empty courtroom, and Wesley couldn't help but suck his breath in. The entire room was finished in shiny, dark-stained wood. The judge's bench commanded the room. It was at least seven feet higher than the courtroom floor. The room exuded power, control, and justice. This, thought Wesley, was why he took this job.

They had to wait about twenty minutes until the arraignment began. Slowly, both court employees and spectators dribbled in. Wesley noted that the first spectators who appeared were the newspaper reporters with their thick notebooks in hand and pencils tucked behind their ears. He asked Day about them.

"They're here every day looking for a story," Day told him. "They're like leeches in a pond. Unfortunately, the politicians that make decisions about our jobs often put more faith in what they write than what we tell them."

Finally, the prisoner was led in and met a well-dressed man at the defense table. The Judge came in, and a bailiff had everyone stand. The man at James' side introduced himself to the court as a public defender assigned to James just for the arraignment. He emphasized the word just.

The judge looked upset and asked the lawyer his name. He replied, "Charles N. Emerson of Pittsfield."

The Judge looked over a pair of spectacles balanced precariously on his nose. It gave him the impression of a schoolmarm about to hand out corporal punishment. "Well, Charles N. Emerson, esquire of Pittsfield, this citizen is charged with three counts of murder. He could face the death penalty. He is indigent and can't afford defense council. So, I, not you, sir, decide who is assigned to what case, and guess what?" There was a grin hidden behind the stern look on the judge's face. "This court orders Charles N. Emerson appointed defense council for the duration of proceedings against," he glanced down at the paperwork, "James Callander."

Emerson looked like he was about to protest, but a single glance from the Judge took care of any protest the lawyer might raise.

The rest of the proceedings were perfunctory, with bond being set at $10,000, and James remanded to jail until the Grand Jury heard his case. Round one went to the lawmen. They made their way back to the District Attorney's office.

Gillett came in a few minutes later. He cautioned them not to underestimate Callander's attorney. He told them that he had seen him in action in court and he was a solid defense attorney even though he obviously wanted no part of this particular case.

Gillett finalized their follow-up assignments and set a meeting for October 15th to see where they stood in uncovering details of the case. With that, he sent the two Sheriffs on their way.

During the ride back to Otis, the two Sheriffs decided that Wesley would work to identify the fishermen that saw

James the morning of the murder at the Pond. Muncie would trace a route between the Pond and the murder scene, talking to farmers and their families to find any potential witnesses. They agreed to meet the following Monday morning in Otis to have breakfast and compare notes.

Chapter Fifteen

Monday, October 6, 1862

Berkshire County Jail

Visitors Room

Lennox, Massachusetts

1:00 PM

Officer Day watched intently as James Callander was led into the visitor room. The District Attorney had requested that Day visit James and see what his state of mind was. Hopefully, he was willing to say something about the case. Callander sat across from Day and looked relatively happy compared to the day he was arrested.

Day started the conversation: "How are you, James? You look good."

"Well, to tell the truth, I haven't eaten this good, ever. I'm actually getting fat." He laughed.

Day smiled. "I know you had a tough life. I can't imagine the obstacles you faced in life."

"You really come here to talk about me? Naw, you are coming to get me to talk about the murder. I got nothin to tell you."

"I sense a but coming, James."

"I know about something else if you're interested?"

"I'm listening, James."

"I want considerations. Maybe more yard time or more food?"

"I can't make promises, James. Doesn't work that way. But, If you help us out, I guarantee we will remember it."

"Better than nothin', I guess. My half-brother, John Henry Guilder, committed rape in Sandisfield last April."

"How do you know this, James?"

"I was with him," James quickly added, "but I didn't do no rape."

"Tell me about it, James."

"This lady, Mrs. Peasley, lived in Sandisfield. Her husband was gone to war. John Henry Guilder and I thought to gratify our passions upon this woman. On April 1st, I accompanied him to her home. We arrived there at about dark. We hid ourselves until she went to bed. Henry, leading the way, we went in through the back into her bedroom. She had a small child in bed with her. She rose up in bed and asked who we were, but we said nothing. Henry pulled the bedclothes up over her head. I stepped up and laid over her head so she wouldn't make any noise. Guilder ravished her and commenced to choke her; she begged us to spare her life for her little child's sake. I told Henry to let her be. He did. We left and returned to my father's place."

"OK, James, I'll look into that. It seems you have a lot of compassion for children. That's why it seems so out of character; you accused of killing two little Jones kids."

"I didn't kill those kids. If you believe anything I've told you, believe that. It's the truth!"

"I think you're trying to tell me something else, James."

"I'm saying nothing else about that. Let's just leave it at that."

"Thank you, James… I'll be back when I check this out."

Day left the jail and immediately went to the stage office. He arranged to have a message delivered to Wesley via the Lee to Winsted stage detailing the new information. He asked Wesley to seek out Mrs. Peasley and verify the story.

Wesley was at home when a young boy delivered the message much later that evening. It was marked urgent. The stage had dropped it off at the Inn, and the youth had been pressed into service to deliver it. Wesley read it through. He wasn't surprised, the entire Callander clan was becoming a giant crime wave. This entire case was growing like a snowball rolling down a hill.

The next morning, Wesley was up and out early. He made his way to the Peasley farm. He was there by 8:00 AM and saw a woman he assumed to be Mrs. Peasley hanging wash on the line as he approached. A small child, a boy of about two or so, was seated on the ground near her laundry basket, playing in the dirt. He had dirt on his face but appeared healthy and contented.

The farm was visibly run down. The weeds were armpit high and almost choked out the lane leading to the house. The buildings needed maintenance and, of course, paint. There were no animals visible, and the entrance to the barn was overgrown with weeds.

The Peasley woman visibly shrank back, seeing a lone male with a badge entering the yard. Alarmed, he was scaring her; Wesley called out to her that he was the Sherriff. That caused her to throw her hand to her mouth and fall to her knees. Wesley quickly dismounted and ran over to her and helped her up. She appeared petrified and hugged him tightly, refusing to let go. The feel of a woman in his arms was unexpectedly pleasant. Then Wesley got it.

"Ma'am, everything is alright with your husband as far as I know."

She began to cry uncontrollably and hung on tightly to Wesley. Eventually, she calmed down and stammered out, "I thought you were here to tell me my husband was dead. Since he left for the war, I've lived in fear that every day someone will be coming to tell me he's dead. His letters are filled with the horrors of this stupid war. He's convinced that he will be killed."

Wesley realized that Mrs. Peasley was young and thin. His arm was around her midsection as he held her from falling, and it sank deeply into the pleats of her dress until it encircled her slim waist. She was very pretty. She was modestly dressed and smelled like rose petals. There was an old, forgotten feeling stirring in his conscious and unconscious that he had to admit he had missed. It didn't help that she clung to him, sobbing, vulnerable, and lonely.

He admonished himself to stop. This poor woman's husband was off fighting a war. He was a better man than that. Yet, he was as reluctant to let go as she was.

Wesley, seeing she was calming down, asked her to sit. "Mrs. Peasley, I have some difficult questions to ask you. Do you feel up to it?"

She simply nodded.

"Last April, did something happen?"

She looked taken aback. Her face blanched, and she immediately looked at the ground. It appeared she wouldn't make eye contact with Wesley again.

Finally, she looked up at Wesley. Tears were forming in the corners of her eyes, and she looked like she was about to cry uncontrollably again. Wesley could almost feel her panic and pain, but he also saw shame, which made Wesley angry. There was no reason for shame. It wasn't her fault that this happened. Wesley chose his words carefully, "I already know most of the story. There is no reason to be afraid or ashamed, Mrs. Peasley. It wasn't your fault. You are the victim. They attacked you."

She looked at him with a blank stare.

"I am simply here to confirm the rest with you. It's ok. Please tell me what happened."

She took a deep breath and looked at him. "Please call me Hope, Sherriff?"

"I'm Wesley... Wesley Langdon."

"Wesley, I am scared." She reached her hand out, took Wesley's hand, and squeezed hard.

"What if they come back? They could have killed me that night. I probably should be dead right now."

"I would never allow that to happen. One is in jail, and the other is not anywhere around here. Don't be frightened."

"I suppose…If you know the story anyway… That night I had gone to bed. The house was dark. I heard someone in my bedroom. I called out, but no one answered. Suddenly the bedclothes were pulled up over my head. Then there was a weight on my head, and someone raped me. When he was done, he started choking me. I begged him to stop. My baby was on the bed next to me, and I begged him not to kill me for my child's sake. A voice further away said, 'Leave her be.' They left. I never saw them in the dark and with the bedclothes over my head. I felt lucky to have survived." She began to cry.

When she calmed down, she stammered, "We had just moved here from Great Barrington in 1861 to start a new life. Calvin, that's my husband, felt it was his duty to fight this war. We argued about it a lot. Don't get me wrong, Wesley, he is a good man, but why leave a family that hadn't even had a chance to exist together just to fight this stupid war? We had just had the baby, and he was gone… just gone. Often, I can't remember him at all. We were only married a little over a year when he left. Then that… happened. It's been like a bad dream.

Wesley sighed. "I can't imagine how hard it was to live through that and then all this time later re-live it again. Hope you're a brave woman. I want you to remember and really believe this wasn't your fault. That's all I need for now. I feel you are perfectly safe with one in jail and the second nowhere around here. I live right down the lane, and I will keep an eye on you. I pray you're safely reunited with your husband soon." Wesley hesitated, weighing what he was about to say. "Look, like I said, I live less than a mile down the road. The farm is on the left. Please get ahold of me if you need anything or if I can be of help."

With that, he mounted up and tipped his hat to the lady. Hope watched him go, holding her baby, looking scared and lonely but at least not ashamed. Wesley admired the spunk in that woman.

Wesley rode back to the inn. He would pen a message to Officer Day, giving him the confirmation of James's story, he was sure he was waiting for. The extended Callander family was turning out to be a crime wave in and of itself. On a hunch, he also penned a note to the Sherriff in Winsted asking him if he knew John Henry Guilder and if he could locate him. Here, for a pleasant change in recent memory, was a living victim he could help.

Over the next week, notes flew between Wesley and Day. An arrest warrant was obtained for Guilder, and through Wesley's efforts, he was located and arrested in Winsted. He was almost immediately bound over for trial by the Grand Jury.

The trial was scheduled quickly. Hope Peasley would have to testify. Wesley made it his personal mission to get her back and forth from Sandisfield to Lennox to prep for and then testify in the trial. A friendship grew between them as the hours together accumulated, but Wesley ensured it was strictly professional. The testimony took a toll on the woman, and Wesley made sure he was there for her to lean on in the tough times. It took a toll on Wesley as well. Maintaining his professionalism became hard. One day, he realized that he had feelings for this woman.

Guilder was convicted in court in record time and sentenced to life in prison. This occupied most of Wesley's time into mid-December. In what moments he had, he continued to work on the Jones murder case. He still found time to occasionally pay a visit to the Peasley farm to help with routine chores.

Wesley wrestled with his friendship with the young Peasley woman. It bothered him. He felt he had cheated on his dead wife and a brave soldier off fighting a war. Yet… he couldn't help but feel something had passed between them in that first moment at her farm. Part of him was uncomfortable with it, yet another was… well… interested. No, far more than interested.

Chapter Sixteen

Thursday, January 1, 1863

Visitor Room, Berkshire County Jail

Lennox, Massachusetts

1:00 PM

Despite herculean efforts by Wesley, Muncie, and Day, the months of October, November, and December had dragged by without a break in the case. They had identified the fishermen that had seen the young colored man by the pond the day of the murder, but none of the fishermen could say for sure (after seeing James) it was him. Muncie had found four witnesses among the local farm community that believed they had seen James that morning, but time had eroded much of the memory and outrage of the Jones tragedy. No one could place James at or even near the Jones farm that day. They had taken a break from the case for the holidays with a big meeting scheduled for mid-January with the District Attorney. Little did Wesley or Muncie know that forces beyond their control had taken a hand in the case.

Reverend Hall had taken Wesley's advice and began volunteering at the Lennox Jail as a spiritual councilor in November. He had taken a special interest in James Callender. They met every time Hall visited the facility, and true to his wish made that September day to Wesley, Hall preached forgiveness through truth to the young man.

Late in December, Callender told Hall that "he and his father had done a bad thing." What followed was a full confession to the Reverend of the murder of Emily Jones and her children. That confession was given to Hall with the provision that it remained only between James and the Reverend, who was James' religious council.

Hall didn't know the law well, but he did know that a confession between clergy and a person he was counseling was privileged and probably wouldn't be admitted in court. It took two more weeks for Hall to convince James that the confession wouldn't mean much unless it brought closure to the rest of the Jones family. Finally, James agreed to talk to the authorities. Hall scrambled about looking for someone in authority to hear the confession, but it was New Year's Eve, and most were out celebrating. On top of that, a heavy snowstorm had clogged the roads slowing travel to a crawl. He was able to find Officer Day, who lived around the corner and who, in turn, located County Coroner Dr. Parsons at his nearby home. He finally got everyone together at 1:00 PM on New Year's Day.

They gathered in the visitor's room, and Day started the conversation. "James Reverend Hall informs me you have something to tell us. Understand that anything you tell us might be used against you in court."

James responded, "Yes, sir, I understand, but we have done something real bad, and I need to tell someone about it."

"Go ahead, James," Hall responded.

"You have to understand right off, we lived for two years in Otis near Mr. Jones an' we got mad at him for accusing us of milking his cows, which was a lie. He also talked to us about drinking rum."

"I started out that day before sunrise. I was supposed to meet my father in Waterman's pasture. I had made an agreement with him that I would creep up Belden's Hill and steal a sheep. I took the town road to Cold Springs at Waterman's Pasture and crossed the bridge by the forge. I went up to the boarding house and got there about sunrise. I went across Hiram Strickland's mowing lot to the old barn of Lewis Clark. From there, I went to the flume of the dam. I found a boat there and went to Cotton Pond. I got to Cotton Pond when the sun was 1-2 hours high. Fished a spell but saw they would not bite and thought I would go to the gulf bridge between the two ponds. I got most way there, and there were some men called to me for a boat. I called out, who called for the boat and took them the boat. I fished briefly, then went down around the Gulf bridge and fished for a few minutes. I crossed the bridge down by the road that goes to Tolland toward the Clark house who lives there. I crossed the road to a lot with a little barn above Cold Springs.

I waited a while and then waded between Amos Cottons' house and Dr. Fox's at Cold Spring. I went across Waterman's pasture and took the old coal route that runs up to the pasture. There I came to where our old cabin used to be where I promised to meet Dad."

James took a breath and continued. "When I was there, he was there, and I said so you got here. He asked what luck? I said Fisherman's luck. I looked up the side hill, saw a woman and two children, and asked who the woman and children were. He told me it was Jones wife and children. I sat down next to Dad, and he took out a bottle of whiskey. We both drank two times.

Then he said, "You know how Jones and his wife talked about us when we lived down in Cold Spring? Now let's have our revenge. I asked him, "Revenge? What do you mean?" Dad said "Let's go down and kill them right now." I said it seemed too bad to kill them, little innocent children, for such a little thing. Dad said It ain't a bit too bad. He took the bottle back out, and we both drank some more. I told him if he would kill the children, I would kill Mrs. Jones."

"We started out and went up the hill. They were above us. We were in a cabin near a swamp. They were about 10 rods from a stone wall. We come up still. She had her back to us, stooping over berry picking. I caught her by both shoulders, grabbed her and threw her down, and sat with my knee in her heart so I could hold her. The children began to cry and scream."

"Seeing me on her, he went to work and killed the children. They were killed first. He picked up a stone and struck the little boy first by the nose and in the forehead somewhere. Then he struck the little girl in the back of the head."

"I had Mrs. Jones down, her clothing up over her head. She did not speak except to say … "Oh dear" and gave me a scratch on the cheek. I shut off her wind. Then he took hold of Mrs. Jones, and I committed rape on her. I then took hold of her on her clothes, and he committed rape. I then picked up a stone and jammed it against her head on top of her clothes three or four times. The stone left my hand each time. I took hold of her body by the upper part and grabbed her clothes around her head like a bag. He grabbed her legs, and we hid her in the roots of a hemlock tree.

We hid the children there, too, but we thought the heap looked too big, and we then hid the children apart and hid Mrs. Jones under a hemlock log and covered her up with leaves. We then picked up some of the berries they had picked, leaves, shoes, and stockings, along with a cap and bonnet, and put them in her tin pail and threw it down the hill. Then Dad and I went down to Erastus Adam's place and got some apples, and I went home."

Officer Day let the silence hang for a moment, then asked. "That it, James?"

"Yes, sir."

Day continued, "Understand, James, we have to check this all out, but I believe you've done the right thing."

Once James was taken back to his cell, Day spoke. "Doctor, does that story match the medical details of your exam on the Jones family?"

"Sir, you cannot believe how many details we uncovered during our investigation that initially stumped us that are now clear to me. By God, Sherriff Langdon had this figured out down to almost every tiny detail that young man just revealed to us. The bigger question here is, do we have enough to get the father? He seemed to me the catalyst that started this whole nightmare."

Day started to organize his thoughts. "I believe we have enough to charge him, and that's a start. Once he is in custody, maybe he will turn out to have a conscience. For now, tomorrow is another day. Reverend, you in town overnight?"

"Yes, staying with the pastor of the Congregational Church here in town. Why?

"Come to the District Attorney's office at 10:00 AM tomorrow. He is going to want to talk to you. Doctor, you took notes while he talked. Go home, rewrite them clearly, and be at that 10:00 meeting as well."

The Reverend and Doctor nodded their ascent, and the three left the jail to finish the holiday.

Chapter Seventeen

Thursday, January 7, 1863

The Langdon Farmhouse

Sandisfield, Massachusetts

7:00 PM

Wesley was adding wood to the stove on a cold January night when the sound of a knock on his farmhouse door startled him. The weather had been terrible. The New Year's Day storm dropped over two feet of snow. In the days that followed, it had warmed into the 40's and the snow quickly melted, turning the roads into impassable quagmires. Then today had been bitterly cold, nearly 20 degrees all day with a strong northwest wind. It froze the muddy roads into rutted nightmares, chasing most folks indoors. The old adage, New England weather, wait a minute, and it changes, was holding true these days. Wesley had heard the stage had finally gotten through this afternoon, although barely.

Wesley opened the door, and there stood a boy, at least he had the face of one, on his stoop. He was cloaked in layers of heavy mismatched clothes that made him look more like a pile of rags rather than a young man. He stood shivering in the frigid night air holding an envelope toward Wesley.

Through chattering teeth, he managed to say, "Letter for you, Sheriff. Came in from Lee on the stage today."

Wesley got the boy in the house, shut the door and pushed him in front of the stove. It was well below zero at this hour, and he could see the boy was freezing. He poured the kid a cup of hot coffee and sat him in a chair to warm up while he read the letter. It was from John Day and detailed James Callender's confession. Wesley felt a little cheated that he had not had a chance to talk to James lately. Perhaps if he had, he would have been satisfied to hear the confession first. He shook off the thoughts, at least there would be closure for the Jones family. He continued reading; the District Attorney wanted him to get to Lennox as soon as the weather allowed. He was told the visit would take some time and to plan to stay for a few days. They needed his help to prepare the case to present to the Grand Jury. Wesley sighed, dreading the trip north in this weather. He would leave in the morning, stopping as necessary to warm himself and his horse along the way.

Meanwhile, the young man had thawed out and was babbling about how the stage had broken an axel on the frozen roads and how the weather was the talk of the town. Weasley listened politely before steering the youth out the door, admonishing him to head directly home. Then he packed himself a bag. He had to stop at the Peasley place on his way out in the morning to make sure she had enough wood split for a week or so. He had been watching out for the young wife since meeting her the previous autumn. No one else seemed to be helping her while her husband was off at war.

The next morning dawned with a thick frost hanging like a white shroud over the Berkshires. The temperature hovered around zero when Wesley walked to the barn to feed, water and saddle his horse. He rode out at about 8:30 AM and went straight to the Peasley farm. Hope Peasley met him at the door and assured him there was more than enough wood for several weeks. One less thing to worry about.

The ride north was a nightmare. As expected, the temperature warmed only into the single digits, and the roads were abominable. His horse had to step slowly and carefully among the frozen wheel ruts so it didn't break a leg. It took over two hours for him to reach Otis, where he warmed up at Dr Spellman's place. He had several ulterior motives, wanting to inform the doctor about James's confession as well as to get some of his wife's great cooking. He left at about noon. He finally arrived in Lennox at eight that evening, thoroughly chilled to the bone. John Day was still at the office and invited him to stay at his place, and a very tired and cold Wesley Langdon accepted without hesitation.

The next day they woke to temperatures below zero. The usually bustling Lennox downtown center was deserted as they crossed the green. They entered the Curtis Hotel dining room for breakfast. It was much different than Wesley was used to. It was opulent instead of the homey country feel of the Days Hotel in Otis. The walls were decorated with wall hangings, oil paintings and sheer drapes. The tables had white linen table coverings, and the waitresses were dressed in uniforms that made them look like maids in a rich man's home. Once they were seated, they feasted on rich dark coffee and eggs benedict, a delicacy you would never find at the Days Hotel in Otis.

Wesley felt almost guilty eating this way, but it was delicious. They lingered over a second cup of coffee before heading for the District Attorney's Office.

The District Attorney's office was abuzz with activity. Secretaries scampered to and fro while the attorneys shouted requests in their direction. The District Attorney was seated at his desk with papers piled high around him. He stood as they entered and shook Wesley's hand warmly and gestured for them to have a seat.

"Sherriff, our gamble with young Mr. Callander paid off handsomely. His confession will ensure a quick conviction, and no politician can second guess our motivation. We also should be able to arrest his father, although, with just his son's word and the current sympathy towards colored folks, I have doubts about the outcome of that part of the case. I have announced we will convene a Grand Jury on March 1st. Hopefully, this wicked weather will have passed by then, so travel will be easier. I hope we can parade both James and Thomas Callander in front of that Grand Jury on the same day. That way, the atrocity is fresh in their mind after hearing James' confession. Hopefully, they can carry that emotion over to Thomas. We have a lot of work to do. When you leave here in three or four days, I want to have prepared all the subpoenas for the witnesses in Otis as well as the arrest warrant for Thomas for you to transport and serve. The sooner we get the father in custody, the sooner we can attempt to break him so that he will also confess."

"Sir, no offense, but I know Thomas," Wesley admonished. "There is little chance he will confess. The best we can hope for is he told someone about the murder, maybe his wife. You think that would be enough to get by the grand Jury?"

"Ordinarily, I would say counting on a wife's testimony against her husband would never happen based on their constitutional rights. This might be a hazy legal situation that falls in our favor. She is white, so she is somewhat protected by law from being forced to incriminate him. He is black and explicitly does not have legal rights under either the U.S. or the Massachusetts Constitutions. That means he is not protected under the color of law. The question might be, is their marriage legally binding in this matter? We will see how this all plays out. I plan to proceed as if they both had all the rights granted under color of law."

"We will have to take it one step at a time, I'm afraid, but I'm hopeful. James will be no trouble in either the Grand

Jury or during the trial. Thomas might be an altogether different story."

With that, they got down to work. Wesley worked with a clerk and a list supplied by District Attorney Gillet to find the addresses of and write out subpoenas for the witnesses needed to testify before the Grand Jury. Day worked with another clerk putting together the arrest warrant for Thomas Callander. Every day, they would meet in the morning, at noon and before they left in the evening to compare notes. Wesley found the work stimulating and the sense of teamwork gratifying.

The evenings at Days' home were filled with discussions about the war, politics and police work. "War" stories of both lawmen's careers were liberally sprinkled in. When Gillet announced on Wednesday, January 13, that all was ready for Wesley to return to Otis, a part of Wesley didn't want it to end.

On Thursday, January 14, Wesley headed south. Day promised to meet him the following Monday, jail wagon in tow, to arrest Thomas in Otis. The ride south was much better than the ride to Lennox had been. The weather had moderated to normal winter weather. It was sunny and bright, with the temperatures in the high thirties. The favorable road conditions let Wesley make the trip home in just over three hours.

He spent that afternoon serving subpoenas. Reverend Hall, Dr. Spellman, and George Jones received one, as well as several other residents who had seen James Callandar the morning of the murder. They needed these witnesses to corroborate James's confession.

It was late afternoon when he finished, and he headed home. The thought of entering a freezing house was too much for Wesley as he passed the New Boston Inn and pulled up for supper and a beer. It was after 9:00 PM when he pulled up in front of his place. Within minutes he had a blazing fire in the wood stove, and he was fast asleep in two hours.

The next day he met the stage with the last subpoena for the fishermen who had seen James at the lake that day. They lived in Winsted, Connecticut, just south of Sandisfield. He included a note for the Sherriff in Winsted requesting that he serve the subpoena and thanked him for all his help in the case. With that, he was free till the following Monday. He headed for the Peasley place to check on Hope and her baby James.

Chapter Eighteen

Monday, January 19, 1863

Day's Hotel

Otis, Massachusetts

7:00 AM

Wesley had left his Sandisfield farm early and was waiting for John Day by 7:00 AM in the dining room of the Days hotel in Otis. Day didn't arrive until almost 10:00 that morning. The jail wagon was quite a bit heavier than a conventional wagon, and the weather had moderated enough that the road melted and became muddy shortly after sunrise. It took considerably longer to make the trip to Otis from Lennox than it normally would on the sloppy surface.

Day had a cup of coffee to warm up before they rode south. After exchanging pleasantries, Day lifted his coat and showed Wesley that he was uncharacteristically wearing a sidearm. He handed Wesley an oilcloth-wrapped package. It contained a holster with a loaded 1860 navy colt pistol in it. Wesley began to protest; it just wasn't his style to be armed. John Day made Wesley take it, explaining that they were only two and Callandar would be riding alone on a third horse on the trip back to Otis. They had to be prepared. They had no way of knowing what Callandar's state of mind would be. He was a big and powerful man. Wesley reluctantly strapped the gun on his waist. They mounted up, the warrant for Thomas Callandar in hand.

The ride to the Callandar shack took concentration on the part of the riders. The road was slick with a coating of thawed mud on top of a rutted, frozen icy base. Prime conditions for a horse to break a leg or slip and throw a rider. The trek was complicated by a third horse in tow, needed to bring Thomas back to Otis. They slowly made their way down the road until the shack was in sight, a thin line of smoke trailing from the stovepipe in the roof. Day brought them to a stop, and, bowing to Wesley's firsthand knowledge of the cabin layout, I asked him how they should proceed.

Wesley's response was immediate. "We ride up to the door and call him outside to ensure he isn't armed. We stay spread out, that way, we make two separate targets if he is stupid enough to be armed. I don't think he will be. Bullying is more his style. He's counting on that to keep James and his wife from implicating him. This will be a shock to him. If he gives us any trouble, we do whatever we need to do fast and hard until he's in irons."

Day thought a moment, "Sounds good to me. You do the talking. You earned this moment."

They rode ahead into the yard. Wesley went right, Day to the left.

Wesley yelled, "Thomas Callandar, officers of the law with a warrant for your arrest. Come out of the house with your hands where we can see them."

There was silence for what seemed like an eternity. Wesley was about to repeat his demands when the door slowly creaked open. Both Wesley and Day instinctually cleared their coats from their guns, their hands resting on the gun butts.

Out of the door first was Thomas' wife, with Thomas cowering behind her. At first, Wesley thought he was going to use her as a shield or hostage, and he tensed. A closer look at Thomas made him relax. He looked terrible. He was as pale as a dark-skinned, colored man could be, bent over coughing with a blanket draped around his shoulders, his hand on his wife's shoulder the only thing keeping him upright.

His wife spoke up. "You, lawmen, take em'. He's bout' dead anyway. I think it's pneumonia. The best place for him is in jail with doctors and all."

Wesley dismounted and cautiously approached the pair. Thomas offered no resistance as he had the hand irons placed on him. Wesley had the wife fetch his tattered coat and had to help Thomas mount the horse. He tied the irons to the saddle horn.

Tomas looked down with half-closed, bloodshot eyes and asked, "Kid talked, didn't he?

"Yes. The warrant is for two counts of murder."

"Kid lied, always lying. I had nothing to do with any of this."

"Plenty of time for talking later, Thomas. Let's get you to a doctor. Wouldn't look good if we arrested you and you died before we got you to jail."

They told his wife where they were taking him, and Wesley promised to stop on his way home and report on his condition. She thanked them and went back into the shack, quietly closing the door behind her. Her demeanor was defeated. A far cry from the defiant woman Wesley had dealt with in September.

On the way back to Otis, they stopped at Dr. Spellman's. He quickly examined Thomas and went to the back of the office, returning with a vile of pills. He gave Thomas one and handed the rest to Day. Day gave him a questioning glance.

Spellman chuckled, "Penicillin, new wonder drug. They have been using it in the war. Fights infection. Should help. He is one sick man. This should help him so he can stand trial."

They finally made it back to Otis and the jail wagon. They transferred Thomas to the wagon, wrapping him in several blankets they had procured from the hotel. The wagon immediately started for Lennox. Day on horseback would catch up easily.

Day turned to Wesley, "Kid, you did a great job on this case. I'm really proud of you. You have a great career ahead of you. See you in Lennox the last week of February. We need all hands on deck for the Grand Jury. I might talk to Mrs. Callandar if I was you. See if she will testify that Thomas was out of the house the morning of the murder. That would cook Thomas's goose."

He shook Wesley's hand and reined his mount northward. Wesley turned southward. On his way home, he stopped at the Callandar shack. Mrs. Callandar opened the door at his knock and ushered Wesley inside. It was dark, with only two candles on a ramshackle table for light. There were no windows, although daylight filtered through a hundred cracks in the walls. In the dim light, Wesley saw the shack consisting of only one large room with three beds pushed against one wall. It had a small sink and hand pump for water in one corner. Heat came from a small, well-used, wood-fired cook stove. Wesley thought that his horse had better accommodations in his barn than these folks did in what they called home. He was beginning to understand their frustration with life.

Wesley explained to Mrs. Callandar that they had stopped at the doctors, and he had given Thomas medicine before taking him to Lennox. He took a great deal of time and effort explaining the legal steps involved in the court process that both Thomas and James would be subjected to. When he was all done, he asked her if she had any questions.

"Sherriff, both my men are in jail in Lennox. For someone like me, Lennox might as well be the North Pole. I got no way to get there. I can't help them. I'm alone, scared and confused. What I don't understand is why, after so long, you came and got Thomas. What happened?"

"James confessed that he and Thomas killed the Jones woman and her two kids. Said he killed the woman after they both raped her. Said Thomas killed those little kids. Confessed first to a preacher and then to the officer that was with me earlier today. I'm sorry."

Wesley looked closely at the woman's face for a reaction. The face was blank.

"Sherriff, what's that mean for my son?"

"I think they will convict him quickly Mrs. Callandar. They may hang him."

Wesley thought he saw a flinch in her face, just a quick sad flicker in her eyes, but in a second, it was gone.

She looked him in the eye. "But they may not?"

"Who can say? Might be better for James if the whole truth came out and the jury could split the blame instead of laying all of it on James' shoulders. You might help out with that."

"What do you mean?"

"When I first talked to you back in September, you told me you couldn't remember if Thomas was home the morning of the murder. I had the feeling you were letting your frustration and hatred answer instead of telling me what you actually did remember. I have to ask you again if you recollect if Thomas was home that whole morning?"

Mrs. Callandar was quiet for almost a minute before answering. "Sherriff, I remember… but how can I choose between letting James hang or letting them both rot in jail… all on what I say! That's the choice you're giving me. Either way, me and my family lose. Would anyone take care of me after being married to a 'colored man'? No, Sherriff, I can't answer your question."

"If they call you before the Grand Jury and you swear to tell the truth, then lie, they will throw you in jail. I don't want to see that happen. You had better decide what the truth really is. I believe they will call you to testify. I am here to help you in any way I can. You only have to ask."

Mrs. Callandar's face remained a neutral mask, but Wesley thought he saw a tear forming in one eye. He felt sorry for her. Wesley said goodbye, promising to stop by occasionally. He mounted his horse and rode south towards home.

He felt the interaction with Thomas and his wife had changed his mindset towards this family. He had a better understanding of how hard it was for them to scrape a living if you could call it that, in a world not of their making.

Chapter Nineteen

Friday, February 27, 1863

District Attorney's Office

Lennox, Massachusetts

4:00 PM

Day, Wesley and District Attorney Gillett were seated in Gillett's office while the DA reviewed the plans for the Callandar cases the Grand Jury would hear beginning Monday, March 2nd. Gillett began by listing the witnesses for James' case.

"First up will be you, Wesley. I need you to establish that there was a murder. Describe the scene and the fact that foul play was evident. That's it. Then the husband goes on the stand to establish the timeline. Next, Doctor Spellman will tell us how they were killed. Then you, Day, lay the foundation for the confession and articulate it. We don't need anything else from you. That should be all the evidence we need to get a true bill. It makes no sense to reveal our whole case before the trial. Questions?"

There were none.

He continued, "With Thomas, a more thorough job is required. The witness list will be the same as in James's case. We need to add Mrs. Callandar, a true wildcard. We really do not know what she will say. If have an indictment on hand for James who knows? That, unfortunately, is far too many ifs for me. We will add Doctor Parsons to reinforce the honesty of James's confession. We must also tell the Grand Jury that Thomas denies any complicity, which worries me.

It all hinges on Mrs. Callandar's testimony. If she admits Thomas was gone the whole morning of the murder, it will add veracity to the confession. Wesley, I think I will ask you to recount in much more detail your investigation into the murder, how it took place and the probability that two people were involved. I will lead you through it with my questions. Make sure not to add things outside the scope of my questions when you answer. It's a gamble but one we have to take. Questions?"

Again, there were none.

"Have we got all of our logistics clear? Doctor Spellman is bringing Mrs. Callander, correct?"

Wesley answered, "Yes sir, all set."

"Good, we will meet here at 8:00 AM Monday morning. Everyone, relax this weekend. We will need to be on our toes for this one."

The weekend passed quickly. Wesley and Day rehearsed their testimony at length until they could recite it without notes. By Sunday night, they were ready. Wesley took a walk to the hotel and called on Mrs. Callandar, who had been put up in a room paid for by the Commonwealth. She ushered him into her room upon his knock.

"How are you, Mrs. Callandar? Comfortable?"

"Sherriff, you were at my place. I never had things this good. First time since September, I've been warm."

"Good. I've arranged a visit after your testimony with both James and Thomas. I know it is impossible for you to get here on your own."

"Thank you, Sherriff, you have been so kind. I hope you will feel the same after tomorrow. You know the position I find myself in. All I ask you is to try to understand."

"If you tell the truth, you won't have any squabble with me, no matter what that truth is."

"Thank you, doesn't seem like a lot, but it is all I got. Now if you don't mind, I need to avail myself of these luxuries that are so fleeting. Good night."

Wesley chuckled as he walked back to Day's place, but secretly, he was concerned. It sounded like Mrs. Callandar was going to save her remaining family rather than James.

Chapter Twenty

Monday, March 2, 1863

Outside the Grand Jury Room

Lennox, Massachusetts

Noon

Grand Jury proceedings were secret by law. No spectators were allowed. Only the 23 jurors, the District Attorney, and, one by one, the witnesses. The witnesses were sequestered before they testified but not after. Wesley and Day waited outside the hearing room after they testified. They anxiously awaited the result of the morning's hearings on James Callandar. The District Attorney exited and announced the Grand Jury was in recess until after lunch. He motioned for the two lawmen to follow him. He walked to his office silently, and when they all were in, he shut the door and smiled grandly.

"They will vote after lunch. The result, in my estimation, is a foregone conclusion. Let's turn our attention to the case against Thomas. Has anyone talked to his wife?"

"I did last night," replied Wesley, "and I'm worried. She told me that when we arrested Thomas, her choices were to say Thomas was home that morning and spare Thomas, or if she admitted he was gone, lost her entire family. Quite frankly, if she did that, she would be homeless without anyone to look out for her. I got the feeling she was going to save whatever part of her life she could."

Gillett asked, "Do we have any evidence to hold over her head? Anything to impeach her testimony if it goes that way?"

They all looked at each other blankly.

Gillett sighed. "I will do my best. Maybe I will have the indictment of her son in my pocket by then. That may sway her testimony. I will also push James's confession and how the crime occurred. All we can do is try."

Shortly after lunch, the Grand Jury returned a true bill against James Callander for one count of murder. The testimony in Thomas' case started midafternoon and continued until 5:00 PM, when they adjourned for the day. Day, Wesley and Gillett met in Gillett's office after the adjournment. Gillett was pleased at how things were progressing but noted the first witness in the morning was Mrs. Callandar. They would know early on what direction the case was going in.

It was a restless night for Wesley. On the one hand, he felt elated that James, who he truly believed killed the Jones woman, was going to trial. On the other hand, he felt the entire crime would never have taken place had Thomas not gotten involved. Now it appeared that Thomas, the most culpable party, might walk away from the punishment Wesley felt he deserved. He realized he had done all he could. Now it was up to the twenty-three citizens seated on the Grand Jury. Wesley finally drifted off to sleep well after midnight.

The next morning dawned cold and clear. The Grand Jury reconvened at 10:00 AM.

For Wesley and Day, the waiting was excruciating. The morning dragged on. Finally, at noon Gillett exited the courtroom, and the three walked wordlessly to his office. Once the door was closed, the District Attorney sat heavily in his chair.

"You were right, Wesley. She saved herself. Said Thomas was home all that morning. I tried ripping her story apart. She as much said James must be lying about Thomas' participation. All we have to rely on now is how the crime took place. This afternoon I'm putting the Coroner back on to stress that the woman was raped multiple times. Then Wesley, your back on the stand to go over how the crime was committed and the likelihood that more than one person had to have been involved. Let's go to lunch."

Wesley was called to the stand at 3:00 PM. Gillett used every Grand Jury trick in the book, leading questions, hearsay, and even Wesley's opinions on how the crime had to have been committed. Wesley thought he had made a compelling case but also realized that the question before the Grand Jury was how Thomas could have been home and committing the murder all at the same time. He finished his testimony at 5 PM as they adjourned for the day.

They met yet again in Gillett's office. The mood was subdued. The District Attorney told Wesley he had done a good job. He would charge the jury first thing in the morning. Then they would wait.

That night John Day and Wesley had a long conversation. Wesley told Day about the conditions the Callandar family endured, and they both wondered why something like this hadn't happened sooner than it did. They agreed that the conditions folks lived in often determined their entry into criminal activity. They agreed that the lives James and Thomas were forced to live were probably as much responsible for the loss of three young lives as were any other factors. While the circumstances the Callanars found themselves living in were sad and regrettable; they did not excuse their behavior. They needed to be punished. Would Thomas literally get away with murder? Only time would tell, but both agreed they had done all they could to see that justice had been served.

The next morning Gillett charged the Grand Jury to reach a decision.

Wesley and John Day passed the time pondering what decision would be reached. As they waited, they discussed how that decision would affect the case. If the Grand Jury did not indite Thomas, he would be released scott free, and in their minds, literally, get away with murder. If the Grand Jury chose to indite him, then much more work would have to go into the case before trial.

They didn't have to wait long. They were summoned shortly before noon. Day and Wesley had to wait while Gillett entered the room to get the verdict. He exited five minutes later.

He looked at the two lawmen and shook his head. "No bill. Thomas is free as of today. He has his wife to thank for that. But we did not fail totally. James will stand trial. As soon as we have a trial date, I will notify you. Thank you both for all your hard work."

Wesley spent his last night with Day. The mood was not festive.

Chapter Twenty-One

Wednesday, June 3, 1863

Berkshire County Courthouse

Lennox, Massachusetts

10 AM

Wesley had been notified via letter that the trial for James Callandar was to begin June 3rd. Jury selection would begin that date with the trial scheduled for June 4th. He had traveled to Lennox on June 1st to prepare for the trial.

Now he was seated, watching the proceedings with interest. He had never been part of a case from start to finish, and now he was watching a trial that his investigation had brought to fruition. He was allowed in the courtroom only because he was not needed to testify. All the witnesses were sequestered.

It was expected to be a capital case, with the Commonwealth asking for the death penalty. In compliance with commonwealth law, there were not one but four judges on the bench, all from the State Supreme Court. They were led by Chief Justice Bigelow. He had associate Justices Dewey, Chapman, and Hoar empaneled with him sitting, shoulder to shoulder, across the elevated bench. They were identically dressed in black robes exuding an aura of authority. The perch, well above the courtroom floor, commanded both the view and respect of the courtroom.

The prosecution was led by Commonwealth Attorney-General Foster, assisted by Berkshire District Attorney Gillett. They were dressed in expensive, matching, dark grey suits, immaculately groomed, and presented a dominating presence. Wesley had met with the prosecution team the two days prior, answering questions and doing errands. He was confident they were ready.

The defense team consisted of Charles N. Emerson of Pittsfield, assisted by N.W. Shores of Lee. Their appearance was more haggard, dressed in mismatched jackets and looking somewhat disheveled. It was hard to imagine, by their appearance only, that they were well prepared. Wesley felt somewhat sorry for them. They really did not have much to work with. Their best bet was to try to get life in prison for James, avoiding the death penalty.

Chief Justice Bigelow called the court to order at exactly 10:00 AM. A pool of 25 potential jurors, all men, in keeping with the law, from throughout Berkshire County, were seated, and voir dire commenced. The process was surprisingly straightforward. Both the prosecutors and defense attorneys questioned each potential juror, asking if they knew of the case, had an opinion on it, or had pre-judged the defendant. The prosecutors asked each if they had an aversion to the death penalty. The first six potential jurors were questioned and placed on the panel. The seventh, Mr. James L. Baker of Pittsfield, expressed that he was a

Christian man who was opposed to the death penalty. He was set aside by the prosecution. The next two joined the jury. The next, H.G. Curtis of Egremont acknowledged he had already reached a conclusion on the case and was set aside by the defense.

The next four completed the process, and by 2PM, they had seated the twelve-man jury. The judge instructed all parties the trial would start at ten sharp the next day.

Wesley stayed in the courtroom after everyone else had left. He marveled at the orderly calm that had prevailed in the courtroom in spite of the conclusion that might be reached. Tomorrow, those twelve jurors would decide the fate of a young man whose life was anything but orderly or calm. Nor was the crime that Wesley was convinced he had committed. He was still troubled that Thomas had escaped punishment, but no one on the prosecution team even mentioned that, nor any future plan to correct that injustice. It was out of his hands now he had done all he could. Wesley shook his head, got up and walked towards Day's home, his head strangely clear for the first time in weeks.

Chief Justice Bigelow's gavel banged down at exactly 10 AM the next day, June 4th 1863. The prosecutor's opening statement, presented by District Attorney Gillett, took exactly ten minutes and gave a quick, orderly synopsis of the government's case.

James Callandar was heard to utter the statement. "That's about it then. It's no use going any further."

Judge Bigelow's gavel banged down sharply. "The defendant will be quiet; no further outbursts will be tolerated." He admonished the two attorneys on the defense team to control their client, or he would remove him from the courtroom.

Attorney Emerson followed with the defense's opening argument, stressing his client was but a pawn and committed only half of the crime. He stressed that Thomas Callandar had got the boy drunk and suggested the crime. The boy was just following his father. What boy wouldn't? Finally, he stressed that his client's story had never changed since his original confession. He explained that this uniformity indicated truthfulness; thus, the story and not just the confession itself was critical in determining the extent of culpability in this case.

Wesley was impressed by this argument, remembering the District Attorney's earlier admonishment not to underestimate Emerson's abilities.

The prosecution opened their case with the victim's husband, George Jones, who laid out the timeline of that fateful morning. He was followed by Doctors Spellman and Parsons, who outlined the victim's wounds and the cause of her death. There was an hour adjournment for lunch at noon.

The trial continued at 1 PM. Reverend Thomas Hall was called to the stand. The defense team immediately jumped up and objected to his testimony. They stated that as he was a man of the cloth, anything their client had told him was privileged information, not admissible in court. Judge Bigelow excused the jury so both sides could be heard.

Once the jury was out of the room, the judge asked the defense to outline their objections.

Attorney Emerson spoke." Your honor, it has been widely held that conversations between clergy and accused are privileged, first in People V Phillips in 1813."

Attorney General Foster countered. "Your honor, the confession Reverend Hall is going to introduce was heard not only by him but in front of the Berkshire County Coroner and a County Court law officer, and only after admonishments that it could be used against him."

"Your honor," interrupted Attorney Emerson, "The original confession was elicited by Reverend Hall while volunteering as a Chaplin in the County Jail. A Chaplin is a man of the cloth by its very nature and definition. That the Reverend was able to convince, maybe even coerce, my client to repeat it to others while serving as a spiritual advisor violates the very tenants of People V Phillips."

The court took a ten-minute recess so the panel judges could discuss the merits of the objection. The judges returned in eight minutes.

Judge Bigelow spoke. "The objection is denied. The defendant, regardless of the spiritual advice or in spite of it, freely confessed to others after being told that anything he said could be used against him. The confession and Reverend Hall's testimony as to his recollection of it will be allowed. Bailiff, bring the jury back in."

Once the jury was seated, Bigelow addressed them directly. "Before you left the courtroom, you heard the defense object to the pending testimony of Reverend Hall. The court has considered the objection and overruled it. The Reverend is allowed to testify, and you will give the same weight to what he says as any other witness."

Reverend Hall recounted the confession exactly as Wesley had heard it. The testimony was devastating for the defense. There were several other minor witnesses who then testified that they had seen James at times and places that corroborated facts in his confession. The prosecution rested.

Judge Bigelow looked at the defense table. "Mr. Emerson, you wish to call witnesses?"

"No, your honor, the defense rests."

"Final arguments then."

District Attorney Gillett stood and quickly recalled what all the witnesses had said, emphasizing the gruesomeness of the crime and James's confession. The result was really a good timeline of events. He left nothing out. He asked the jury for a guilty verdict.

Attorney Emerson rose slowly from the defense table for the defense team's closing arguments. "Gentleman of the Jury, the prosecution has presented a strong case. I want you to remember Reverend Hall's testimony. My client told him that this entire crime was thought of and suggested by his father… Not James."

He paused for emphasis. "His father got this boy intoxicated to lower any inhibitions this youth had. His father beat to death the two defenseless children. Not James. James's story has not wavered in its details one iota in its retelling since he first confessed. To me, that tells me that James is telling the truth, and isn't that what we are doing here today, trying to uncover the truth? I ask you to weigh these facts as you deliberate this case. Who is really to blame here? What degree of culpability does James shoulder, as opposed to his father, in this macabre story? This boy who, as he was taught to do his entire life, listened to his father. Thomas Callander, who suggested the crime. Who then had a greater role in this gruesome event? I would suggest that the evidence must lead you to conclude that Thomas Callander, and not James Callander, masterminded these events. You must consider this when you deliberate this young man's fate."

Attorney Emerson slowly turned and tiredly returned to the defense table and sat down heavily.

Judge Bigelow then instructed the jury as to the elements of the crime and how they were to proceed. The jury was dismissed to the deliberation room, and the court was in recess. It was 2:30 PM.

A reporter from the Berkshire Eagle who had covered the trial all that day wrote as he closed out his column to meet the deadline for afternoon publication. "We are compelled to suspend our report here. The trial will probably close tonight with a verdict of guilty."

The reporter's instinct was correct. The jury returned at 5:00 PM. Once the court was reconvened, Bigelow asked the jury foreman if they had reached a verdict.

The Jury Foreman, Mr. F.W. Gibbs of Lee, answered. "Yes, your honor. We have."

"The Defendant will stand. What say you, Mr. Foreman?"

"We, the jury, find the defendant… James Callandar… guilty of one count of murder."

"Thank you all for your service. You are dismissed. Everyone else 10 AM tomorrow for sentencing. The prisoner is remanded to the County Jail."

He banged the gavel down, stood, and all the justices exited the courtroom.

Wesley again waited until the courtroom was empty. By his count, the entire trial had lasted eight hours. It seemed so perfunctory. It was such a short time with minimal information presented that now held a man's life in the balance.

The next day, punctual as always, Judge Bigelow banged his gavel at exactly 10 AM. Today instead of looking calm, he looked nervous, as if a great weight were upon his shoulders.

"Mr. James Callandar, you have, by your own accord, confessed to this horrible crime. In just a few moments on that Sunday, September last, you not only took a human life but tore asunder a loving family. It matters not under the color of law that you may have been enticed to kill this woman by liquor and your father's influence. You made the choice yourself. You could have walked away from the entire event before it happened. Otherwise, Mrs. Jones and her two children may be here today. You did not. Please stand, Mr. Callandar. Do you have anything to say before I pass sentence?"

James looked at the floor and shook his head no.

"Mr. James Callandar, in accordance with the laws of the Commonwealth, this judicial panel has voted that you shall be hung by the neck until you are dead. The date of the execution of this sentence is to be determined by the County." Looking directly at James, his face softened, "May God have mercy upon your soul. This court is dismissed."

Wesley sat there, his mouth open. His work, their work, days upon days, hours upon hours of it all came down to that three-minute speech by the Judge. James was going to die. Thomas was a free man. Wesley wasn't sure how he felt about any of that. All he knew was that it was done, and all he wanted was to go home.

Chapter Twenty-Two

Wednesday, June 24, 1863

New Boston Inn Taproom

Sandisfield, Massachusetts

5:00 PM

It had been almost three weeks since the Callandar trial, and Wesley had busied himself doing chores on both his and the Peasley farm. He had painted fences and barns, mucked stalls, spread manure and plowed medium-sized gardens on each farm, planting them with vegetables that were now growing well. The physical labor felt good after the mental struggles of the case and trial. Frankly, Wesley still hadn't reconciled himself to the trial's outcome, particularly the sentence it imposed. It gnawed at him.

His life, however, was settling into a quiet, comfortable rhythm. Although taxing, the upkeep of two farms seemed to release his anxiety over the results of the Jones murder case. He had time to reconnect with people in town once again. Life returned to some of its normal routines.

This day, early in the summer season was warm with bluebird skies. It was the kind of weather that helped to release all the shadows that encumber one's soul. With that mindset, Wesley took a ride into town to see people and catch up on the town news. He rode up to the New Boston Inn and strode thirstily into the cool establishment. He entered the inn and smelled the unmistakable aroma of beef cooking.

The proprietor, Danial Brown, greeted him warmly. "Sherriff, you saved me from sending my son to fetch you. I have something to show you… but later. First, a cold beer and then a grilled steak. Just got a load in from the butchers."

"Dan, you can read minds. That sounds so good. Long time since I had a relaxed, calm, quiet dinner."

The dinner was delicious. A thick steak, perfectly medium rare, roasted potatoes crisp on the outside, moist and steaming on the inside and roasted root vegetables that were caramelized in their own juices, drizzled with maple syrup. Topped off with a few cool beers, it was as good as it got, gastronomically, in the Berkshires.

After he had finished his dinner, Brown came over to Wesley and motioned him over to a vacant table, well away from other patrons. After they were seated, Brown held out an envelope. It was addressed to Hope Peasley. The return address was from Lt. Colonel Joseph B. Parsons, 10th Massachusetts Infantry, Army of the Potomac.

Wesley looked at Brown, confused." What is this, and why am I holding it?"

"Look… Sherriff, I know you've helped out the Peasley woman this winter, and I thank you for that. She doesn't know many in town and really was left alone when her husband went off to fight. I act as the Postmaster for

Sandisfield, and I see all of the mail that comes in. I've delivered the many letters Calvin Peasley writes his wife. This is not from her husband. I have a bad feeling about what's in this letter. It looks like it's from his commanding officer. I have been concerned of late.

There have been no letters from Calvin over the last three weeks. That is totally unlike him. He's written at least once a week since he left for the war. Those two facts disturb me. I don't want to just give this letter to her, if it is what I think it is, and leave her alone. Could you bring it to her? You are about the closest friend she has in town. She might need someone with her when she opens it."

Wesley looked at the envelope as if it had a disease. The carefree feeling that had brought him to town vanished instantly. It was replaced by a myriad of different feelings, which swirled through Wesley. His proximity, when he assisted with Hope's farm chores, had fostered feelings between them. Wesley had taken great pains maintaining a non-emotional, purely plutonic distance between them. That was not to say he didn't feel some attachment to the woman. Their relationship, even as friends, was going to make it awkward delivering the news of her husband's death if, indeed, that was what this was.

On the other hand, the news might clear the table for him to step into the emotional void. Did he really want that? Part of him hated the idea. It was like stealing from the dead.

But… there was a part of him that relished the opportunity. He picked up the envelope and headed home. Tomorrow he would ride out and face what came. He owed it to Calvin Peasley and would stand tall for his friend Hope Peasley, no matter the news.

The next morning, he headed towards the Peasley farm. The Hall family owned the neighboring farm just to the south of the Peasley place. Wesley knew them in passing but not much better. He took a chance and stopped to talk to 62-year-old Lorilla Hall, the matriarch of the Hall clan.

He knew Lorilla by reputation. She often took the younger wives in the area under her wing, helping them through the various domestic and child-rearing issues that arose in the isolation of the Berkshires.

Lorilla was a typical 62-year-old Berkshire farmer's wife. When she answered the door at Wesley's knock, she was wiping her hands on a colorful, handmade apron. She stood maybe five feet tall. Time and birthing four children had caused her waistline to expand. She was what some would call pleasantly plump. Her face was framed by salt and pepper hair that was cut short, no doubt a utilitarian effort to keep it out of her way but still radiated a mother's calming aura. Wesley immediately understood why younger women looked up to her. Once Wesley explained his mission to Lorilla, he asked if she would be willing to step in if the news in the letter was as bad as he feared. She acquiesced immediately. Wesley promised to let her know either way.

He continued down the lane to the Peasley farm. Hope heard the horse and met him on the front porch.

"Wesley, good to see you…. What's wrong… you look terrible?"

Wesley slowly and deliberately dismounted and tethered his horse.

He walked up to Hope and, with knots in his stomach, slowly began. "Dan Brown over at the Inn gave me a letter to bring to you. He is worried it might be bad news. He knew I was helping you out and asked me to bring it. So, if it is… bad news… you wouldn't be alone. I pray it is not, but there is only one way to find out. Here." Wesley handed her the letter.

Hope brought her hands up to her face. A look of anguish started on her face.

"Hope, we know nothing for sure. Read the letter. I'll wait by the barn."

She sat on an old, rickety chair on the porch and held the letter with both hands as it rested in her lap, staring at it for a long time. Finally, she rose and took it into the house. Wesley started splitting firewood. He had just split the first log when he heard a wail from inside the house. Hope came staggering out into the yard, the open letter held against her bosom, tears streaming down her face, and she fell to her knees in the mud. She was sobbing uncontrollably and, in between sobs, trying to catch her breath. Wesley rushed to her side, picked her up and helped her into the chair.

"Hope, what is it? What does it say?"

She was choked with emotion and simply held out the sheet of paper. Wesley took it and read it quickly. There were only three short paragraphs. Calvin had been killed during the Battle of Chancellorsville in Virginia on May 5th. The commanding officer sent his condolences. He was buried in a cemetery near the battlefield. Calvin was gone.

He looked at Hope to find her staring at him questioningly through her tears.

"What will happen to me, my baby…, and the farm?" She wailed.

He had to look away.

"Hope, I am so sorry. I never knew Calvin, but I could tell he was a good man, stepping up to fight for his country. He chose you; I'm sure you and little James were on his mind when he died. He loved you both. Now is not the time to worry about all those other things. You need to grieve and remember."

Wesley heard a buckboard behind him and saw Lorilla Hall being driven by one of her sons coming quickly towards them. True to form, she had anticipated the worse. She dismounted, took in the scene with a glance and took charge. She took Hope by the hand and took her into the house, ignoring Wesley.

A few minutes later, they came out of the house, Hope carrying the baby.

"They are going to stay with us at our place until all this gets straightened out. You," pointing at Wesley, "figure out what needs to be done here on her farm and get it done. If you need help, stop by. My boys are glad to help."

With that, Lorilla pushed Hope up into the buckboard, and they were off in a cloud of dust down the farm lane.

Wesley didn't know what to do next. Competing emotions were fighting a pitched battle within him. Hell, did he even know what he felt or what he should feel? He just turned away and started walking, tears staining his cheeks. He knew what it was like to lose someone you loved. He felt so bad for Hope. Nothing anyone could do or say would fill the void she felt right now. Only time would help, and then not much. He walked out into the overgrown meadow, sat down and stared at the morning sun for hours, feeling sorry for Hope, Calvin, maybe even James Callandar, and himself. This, he thought to himself, was not going to be easy for him, Hope, and the folks that attached themselves to all of them.

Chapter Twenty-Three

Thursday, October 1, 1863

Langdon Farm

Sandisfield, Massachusetts

9:00 AM

It had been almost four months since Hope Peasley had received the news of her husband's death and over five months since the Callandar trial. News had come from Lennox right after the first of July that the execution date for James Callandar had been set for November 12th.

Wesley's emotional state was still… not in a stable place. Hope had been welcomed to stay with the Halls until she decided on what was going to happen. He had taken Sunday supper over there almost every week to be with Hope yet was still unsure of his feelings for the woman. Wesley had a feeling, although it was never verbalized, that Hope was waiting for him to make a decision. They often walked down the lane to his or her farm on those Sunday evenings, talking about everything except the future. They became good friends for sure, and these were pleasant days for Wesley. The company of a warm, caring woman brought back wonderful memories. Outside of Sunday evenings, he avoided even thinking about the future. Instead, throwing himself into both his and the Peasley's place. They needed a lot of attention, and it felt good to be farming again.

It kept him from facing the decisions that loomed. Then there were a few law enforcement issues that arose from time to time that he had to deal with. These he found the most fulfilling, and he wondered if the law enforcement life could work with family life.

This morning, he was at his farm cutting down the high grass and weeds along the fence lines in preparation for whitewashing the fence. The morning was quite warm for early October, and he had just taken a break, leaning on the long scythe letting the sweat that soaked his shirt dry in the warm air. He looked up and saw a plume of dust approaching. As it got closer, he saw that it was caused by the son of Dave Brown, the owner of New Boston Inn, riding his horse hard up the lane.

He pulled up in a swirl of dust. "Sherriff, a message came by the stage. They were flagged down on the way down here. They want you right away at the Cold Springs iron works. Woman up there hurt mighty bad."

Wesley's interest was piqued. "On my way."

He headed for the barn and saddled his horse. He stopped at his house only to change his shirt, grab his badge and a hat before riding out. In half an hour, he was at the ironworks.

The owner, Henry Mellis, met him at the door to the office. "Sherriff, it's Mrs. Callandar. Thomas beat her badly. She crawled on her own down here to get help. Doc Spellman is on the way. It's bad."

Wesley walked into the office to find Mrs. Callandar lying on the floor covered with a blanket, and despite the warm temperatures, she was shivering in shock. Both eyes were blackened, and she was bleeding from split upper and lower lips. She tried to move but moaned loudly at the effort. There was no telling how bad the damage that was hidden under the blanket might be.

"She looked up at Wesley through bloodshot eyes. "Sheriff, I lied to the Grand Jury. Thomas was not home at all the morning of the murders. I told him I was going to tell you. I can't let my boy hang without trying to save him. Thomas didn't like that much." She started to chuckle, but it ended with a coughing fit that brought blood spitting from her mouth.

It was obvious she was in a lot of pain. "Mrs. Callander, rest now. Doc Spellman's on the way. Time enough to talk later. Where did Thomas get to after… this?"

"Stormed out. Haven't a clue where he goes. He was roaring drunk and damned mad. You be careful if you're going after him."

The door opened, and Dr. Spellman entered. "Sherriff," he nodded as he looked at the woman, "Take yourself out of here and guard the door till I see what I've got here. If I need help, I'll call."

Wesley left as the doctor rolled up his sleeves and knelt next to the woman.

Outside, he questioned Henry Mellis to see if he could get any other details that would help him. Henry could add little. It was clear that Mellis had probably saved the woman's life. Wesley thanked him and asked him to help the doctor if he asked.

Wesley went to his horse and untied the saddlebag. He pulled out the 1860 Navy Colt pistol that John Day had given him many months before. He checked it was properly loaded and strapped it on his hip. If he found Thomas, he probably would need it. He mounted up and headed to the Callandar place.

On high alert, he rode up the lane towards the shack, but all seemed quiet. The door hung by one hinge twisted at an unnatural angle. He watched carefully for movement but saw none.

Wesley stopped well back from the shack and called out. "Thomas, Sherriff Wesley Langdon, if you're in the cabin, come out with your hands where I can see them."

There was no answer, movement or noise from the cabin. Wesley dismounted and, drawing his pistol, approached the cabin cautiously. Instead of going directly to the door, he flattened himself against the front peering through the numerous cracks and chinks in the cabin. It was dark, but he detected no movement or noise at all and cautiously approached the door. He entered quickly, moving out of the light streaming in from the door so he wasn't skylighted against the opening. His eyes adjusted quickly, and he saw that the cabin was in shambles.

The beds were thrown about, bedding stained with blood piled in the middle of the floor. Pots and pans were all over the cabin. In short, it was a mess, but it was empty. Wesley went outside and walked slowly and quietly around the cabin, trying to find a direction where Thomas might have gone. He encountered bloody drag marks where Mrs. Callandar crawled towards the ironworks but found no sign of Thomas.

Frustrated, his emotions boiled over, and he screamed," Callandar, you coward. You beat women, do you? I'm here now. Come on out and pick on somebody your own size."

The words just echoed off the hills, and no response followed. Wesley immediately felt like a fool. He was much more professional than that. Thomas could wait. Time to do his job. He mounted up and trotted his mount briskly back to the Iron Works.

Doctor Spellman was supervising the loading of Mrs. Callandar into the back of his buckboard as Wesley approached.

Before Wesley could speak, Spellman told him, "She's got a broken arm, several broken ribs and some internal bleeding. I think she will live, but I could be wrong. That animal beat her within an inch of her life. No one deserves this. It will be weeks before she can testify... she told me all about her lies. Sherriff, I don't often get mad, but when you get the warrant, please come get me. I'll gladly help you serve it with my shotgun! I'm bringing her to my place to recover. Come see us in a day or two, and I'll know more. You best get to Lennox. I expect you have a bunch of paperwork to do up there. You are a good man, and by my reckoning, you might have a second chance at justice for the Jones kids. Do what you do best. God's speed."

With that, he climbed aboard the buckboard. Mr. Mellis was in the back, holding Mrs. Callandar steady. The doctor drove slowly and deliberately as he headed towards his place. Wesley admired both men's compassion. He headed home to pack a bag. He could still make Lennox before dark. An hour later, he was heading towards Lennox on the road between Sandisfield and Otis.

Chapter Twenty-Four

Thursday, November 5, 1863

District Attorney's Office

Lennox, Massachusetts

9:00 AM

Wesley had spent a lot of time in Lennox since Mrs. Callandar had told him Thomas was not at home the morning of the murder. The first order of business was to get Thomas arrested for beating his wife. Wesley applied for an arrest warrant. In deference to the travel capabilities of Mrs. Callandar for a trial, it was held back, finally being issued on November 6th.

The doctors had cleared Mrs. Callandar to travel on the first of November, but she was still pretty banged up with her right arm in a sling. Sherriff Muncie had brought her to Lennox on November 4th so she could testify before the Grand Jury.

Today, Mrs. Callandar was slated to present her testimony before a newly seated Grand Jury. This was the second attempt by the Commonwealth of Massachusetts to indite Thomas Callandar for the murder of the two Jones children. According to District Attorney Gillett, their chances were better than the first time around, but, not a sure thing.

Wesley was seated in the District Attorney's office, going over his testimony with Mr. Gillett. It was going to be a complicated case. Gillett explained that double jeopardy didn't apply in a Grand Jury indictment, only in a courtroom case.

They had a second chance at Thomas Callandar. When he took the stand, Wesley's first job would be to tell the story of the case. That was the easy part. The rest would be tough. He had to apply common sense and reason to explain why Mrs. Callandar was recanting her testimony to the first Grand Jury. She openly admitted that she had committed perjury the first time she testified. Somehow, he had to make the jurors believe her testimony this second time. Not an easy task.

Attorney Gillett felt this was a second chance they never expected to have and didn't want to overlook anything in an all-out effort to bring justice to the Jones family. Wesley couldn't agree more. Wesley, the two doctors, Mrs. Callandar and even James Callandar, were slated to testify. They would know soon if their efforts would be rewarded.

The Grand Jury convened at 10:00 AM sharp. Wesley was a witness and sequestered before his testimony, but John Day, as assistant to the District Attorney, was in the courtroom for the whole proceeding. He related what had occurred to Wesley at 4 PM, outside the courtroom, as the Grand Jury began deliberations.

"Wesley, you did a remarkable job with your testimony. You showed the Grand Jury that the crime had to have been committed by two persons. That had to be an enormous swing in their understanding of the crime. Then with more empathy than I could have ever brought, you described Mrs. Callandar's family situation. Your deconstruction of the dilemma facing Mrs. Callandar when testifying the first time, with the impact each decision would have on her life, was riveting. You could not have done more.

Mrs. Callandar's testimony was, or at least seemed, very honest. She admitted she had lied to the previous Grand Jury by saying her husband was at home the entire morning of the murders. She then testified that Thomas was not at home that morning. She then said that Thomas had told her one day, long after the murder, while in a drunken state, that he had killed the Jones children, not James. That was the first time any of us had heard that from her lips. Gillett reminded her that she could get arrested for perjury by admitting she lied the first time before the Grand Jury. Her answer was exquisite. She said she was petrified for her future the first time but now realized the truth would set her free no matter the consequences. The Grand Jury sat up straighter when she said that. It had an impact. Whether they believed it or what the discussions in the jury room centered on during deliberations is really the crux of the case."

Wesley interrupted, "Mrs. Callandar is a conflicted soul. Her life is simple and hard. All she was trying to do was hang on to something, anything that she could. I hope the Grand Jury saw that. That conflict would have broken most women. I admire her courage.

Day answered, "I hope they did. It was there to be seen and understood.

Day continued, "The doctor's testimony was pretty much boilerplate from the first hearing. The real surprise was James Callender's testimony. He repeated his confession verbatim from the first day he told it. It was as if he emphasized his father's parts in it. There was almost a hatred I detected in his testimony.

That may have hurt us. Gillett asked him why he was testifying against his father. He admitted that he was guilty of killing Mrs. Jones, but his father had not only killed the two children, but he had also suggested the whole affair. James felt if he had to die for his small part in this, his father should be hanged for thinking the whole thing up."

After hearing the recap of the testimony from Day, Wesley felt good. Mrs. Callandar's new and sudden revelation that Thomas had confessed to her bothered Wesley. Why hadn't she mentioned it earlier? It almost sounded like she was trying too hard to save James. If he thought this, what was the Grand Jury thinking?

All the cards were on the table now. The Commonwealth had presented the whole story to the Grand Jury. It was now in their hands. It had been two hours so far with no decision. Gillett stopped and talked to them and seemed upbeat. He explained that the Grand Jury could have dismissed the case outright, but they hadn't. Instead, they were deliberating the multitude of facts they had heard. This was heartening. They just had to wait, and wait, they did. The Grand Jury adjourned at 6 PM without a decision. It reconvened at 10 AM the next morning but sent a representative out at 11:00 AM to ask the District Attorney several questions. Before returning to their deliberations, they wanted clarification on various pieces of testimony and points of law. Wesley and John Day went to lunch at noon with no decision. It wasn't until 5 PM that they received word that the Grand Jury had ruled.

Day and Gillett entered the room, and it was, in accordance with the law, sealed. Wesley was forced to wait outside. He couldn't sit still but paced up and down the corridor for twenty minutes. It was 6:15 PM when the door swung open, and Gillett and Day exited.

Day indicated Wesley should follow them as they walked wordlessly back to the District Attorney's Office. They entered and closed the door. Gillett opened his desk drawer and pulled three glasses and a bottle of whiskey. He proceeded to pour three fingers into each glass. Wesley was still in the dark. Gillett handed each man a glass, raised his, and said, "We fought the good fight, one of the best I've been involved in. I toast your professionalism, efforts, and, most of all, your drive for justice. To you, gentlemen." With that, he raised his glass in a toast to the lawmen.

Wesley drank but was still not sure what was happening. Finally, he couldn't stand it anymore. "What the hell happened in there?"

It was Day that answered. "Wesley, they refused to issue a true bill. They told us that they just didn't trust Mrs. Callandar's motives. They thought she might be lying to try and save the son." Wesley's shoulders slumped, and he sat heavily.

Gillett continued, "You did a good, no a magnificent job testifying and throughout this messy case's investigation. We all did our best, but the justice system has spoken. Doubtless, we won't get a third chance. It's over."

Wesley put his glass down, stunned. Gillett refilled all three. "We need and deserve another."

After they drank, Gillett said, "Wesley, I'm sure you want to go home, but please indulge me and meet me here tomorrow morning. I want to rehash this business with you."

Wesley just nodded numbly. He didn't know how he felt or how he should feel.

At 9:00 AM the next morning, he was back in Gillett's office. Gillett got up from his desk. "Wesley, a year ago, I didn't know you. Today I see sitting before me a Sherriff with whom I would trust with any case, any circumstance, any challenge. Moreover, I see a friend and colleague. You, sir, should be proud of your work. The people of southern Berkshire County are fortunate to have you."

Wesley was embarrassed. "Sir, we lost. Thomas Callandar will get away with murder."

"Wesley, we did our level best with the cards we were dealt. In fact, we squeezed every last ounce out of the facts we had and almost pulled it off. It was a near thing. The law prohibits me from revealing all the Grand Jury deliberations, but I can tell you one vote separated the jurors from issuing a true bill. We did our best. You, sir, went above and beyond your best. Go home. No regrets. The justice system has spoken, and we all know justice is often blind. If I can ever do anything, you get ahold of me. I mean that, sir."

They separated with a sincere handshake. Wesley went outside to where John Day waited with his horse.

"Wesley, it has been an honor to work with you. If you ever need anything… you get hold of me. You keep up the good work."

They started to shake hands but ended up in an embrace.

"Be safe, Officer John Day."

"You as well, Sherriff Wesley Langdon."

Chapter Twenty-Five

Saturday, November 14, 1863

Taproom, New Boston Inn

Sandisfield, Massachusetts

9:00 AM

The bar at the New Boston Inn was not usually open at nine in the morning, but Dave Brown had opened for Wesley so he could meet the early stage from Lee. Word had been passed to him that James Callandar had been hanged on November 12. Wesley had purposely not attended, although the High Sherriff thought he should show up for publicity reasons. Wesley felt that justice, in this case, had not been fully realized. He didn't want his personal stamp of approval inferred from the results by attending the execution. In his eyes, the case would never be closed.

Yet Wesley's curiosity had gotten the better of him. What had happened that fateful day on the gallows in Lennox? Wesley had asked the stage drivers to quietly bring him the local newspaper, The Berkshire County Eagle, published in Pittsfield, which had covered the execution in detail. The stage drivers lived up to their word and had dropped off the paper an hour earlier. Now Wesley was at the bar, with a fresh, strong cup of coffee in front of him as he read the paper.

The article was long. It consisted of not only the entire front page but most of the second page. The first few paragraphs were a recap of the crime, which Wesley found very factual. It was followed by James' confession from his trial. Unfortunately, it also recapped James' confession in the Peasley rape matter. That would raise bad memories for Hope. He would have to keep the article from her.

There was a short biography on James which Wesley found interesting. This was one area he had not been involved in during the investigation. It listed little education, family or religious life, and one could sense the reporter was using it to paint James as an evil man. James did not help his cause. The reporter related that James expressed little remorse when speaking with his spiritual advisors prior to his execution, nor did he as he stood on the gallows. The press used all of this information to paint him as a monster. Wesley was immediately puzzled about how the press had access to what transpired between a condemned man and his spiritual advisor. Still, he remembered the tenacity of reporters at the court building when during James' arraignment. The reporter noted that James' mother, Mrs. Callandar, had visited James the day before he was hung. That made Wesley glad.

The paper reported that High Sherriff Root had allowed reporters into the jail to interview both James and Thomas. The interview with James was interesting. The facts in his confession delivered the day before he was hung to the reporter were identical, almost word for word, from his first confession on January first. All the more, that convinced Wesley that Thomas was getting away with murder. Wesley was glad that James made sure the reporters knew he was angry with Thomas. James made it crystal clear that Thomas was much more to blame than him. In spite of this, James never once denied his own guilt. James told the reporters that during his months in jail, he'd hoped Thomas might confess to his part in the crime. James had hoped such a confession might be a cause for him to be pardoned from a death sentence. Wesley thought about this, and given the abolitionist stance of the Governor, a pardon would have been a good possibility.

The interview with Thomas, who was arrested the day before the execution on Wesley's warrant, and was now in jail for beating his wife, was a real inquisition by the reporter. They came right out and accused him of lying about the murder, throwing his wife's new testimony in his face. Thomas held steadfast to his innocence, although lamenting that he was sad to see his son hang. Thomas came across as shallow and a liar. Wesley was pleased with the portrayal.

According to the article, James was led up onto the gallows at 10:20 AM on November 12, 1863. His father, Thomas, was purposely put in a cell a stone's throw away, overlooking the gallows, and was forced to watch the execution. High Sheriff Root read the warrant for James' execution and asked him if he had anything to say. James replied, "No, I have not much to say. I wish to say my father got me into this scrape. He got me full of rum and then left me to hang while he was not. That is my story, and I would stick to it even as this is the last day of my life."

Thomas yelled through the cell window, "James, how can you die with such a falsehood in your mouth."

Thomas was about to say more, but Sherriff Root commanded him to stop.

James replied, "It's the truth."

Sherriff Root then stated, "May God have mercy on your soul."

Root pressed the release with his foot. James fell ten feet. After three minutes, his pulse went to 120, and after five minutes, there was a slight tremor.

After ten minutes, the body was cut down and sent to the medical college in Lennox for study.

The article went on to say that the father of Emily Jones and George Jones, the victim's husband, was present at the execution. They noted that George Jones seemed distraught at the scene. The reporter surmised that George Jones "undoubtedly recalled vividly to mind the terrible ordeal through which he had been called to pass." Wesley thought the reporter really had no clue what he had gone through.

The article also noted Mrs. Callandar had been arrested. Of course, Wesley knew this was the arrest for perjury before the Grand Jury. He had been told that the District Attorney would sentence her to time already served in jail and then release her. She had been through enough.

Wesley put the paper aside for a second and sipped his coffee. He was still trying to sort out his personal feelings about the whole affair. He had to admit; he'd been drawn into the social dilemma that was the Callandar family's daily life. It no doubt contributed to their involvement in the whole sordid affair. He felt he understood some of the forces and prejudices that had been at work and wondered if it was the same for other free colored families that lived in the North. It seemed to Wesley that their hopes and dreams were in direct opposition to the reality the conservative white folks living in Berkshire County practiced.

Wesley went back to reading the article. The last sentence of the final paragraph caught him by surprise. It read: "The duties of Sherriff Root, though most painful and embarrassing, it being the first scene of that kind he had been called upon to participate, were performed with perfect coolness and presence of mind, showing that in the position of Sherriff, Berkshire has... The right man in the right place."

Wesley re-read the paragraph three times. Damn, the politics! He stood up, drained his remaining coffee, placed the cup on the bar with a dollar and walked out, pausing only long enough to deposit the newspaper in the fireplace, where it belonged. It flamed quickly as it hit the hot coals. Wesley recalled the words spoken at burials, ashes to ashes, dust to dust. Ashes, a fitting end to the whole episode. It was time to go home and make some life-changing decisions.

Chapter Twenty-Six

Saturday, May 7, 1864

Dining room, New Boston Inn

Sandisfield, Massachusetts

Noon

Wesley sat at the head table, watching his guests as they twirled and danced to the local three-piece band. Hope was seated to his right. Things were good on all fronts. The Union was beginning to win the war, and the casualty lists in the local papers were slowly shrinking. It had been a fairly mild winter and a benign spring with plenty of water. The crops were being sown with an optimism that belied the reality of Berkshire farming.

Hope turned to Wesley smiling and said, "Hope Langdon has a very nice ring to it, doesn't it?"

"I hope you know what you're getting yourself into. There is a lot that goes with that name, Mrs. Langdon."

Hope just laughed. It was nice seeing her relaxed, happy and laughing. Despite Wesley's misgivings, one day last December, they had finally sat and talked about the future. The closing of the Jones murder case had lifted a weight from Wesley.

It allowed Wesley to do some hard thinking and personal self-evaluation. The result was Wesley's honest outpouring of his feelings about farming, being Sherriff, and loneliness.

Hope was equally honest and had, at length, talked about her marriage with Calvin and how brief it had been. When they were done, they both smiled and agreed that simply talking about it had brought them much closer. That day, Wesley thought that Hope's smile was one of the best things he had ever seen. More time together and deeply personal conversations led to today's wedding. Wesley finally felt content with who he was and how his life was playing out. It was a good and powerful feeling.

With Hope's blessing, they had deeded most of the old Peasley farm to the Hall family in thanks for keeping Hope and James for the better part of a year. Their oldest son and his new wife were moving in. Life moved on. Wesley did keep two big pastures near the back of the former Peasley place that directly adjoined his... no... it was now their land. Good-haying pastures, for sure.

The District Attorney of Berkshire County, Ward B. Gillett, had presided over the wedding ceremony and now found his way to the head table.

"Wesley and Hope, you make a perfect couple. The paperwork you requested to adopt young James has been fast-tracked in the courts. It should be done by June first. All you need to do is come up to Lennox and sign off, but it's just a formality."

"Thank you, sir," replied Wesley.

Hope got up and hugged him, then kissed him on the cheek, causing the Berkshire County District Attorney to blush noticeably.

John Day, who had stood up for Wesley as his best man, strolled up. Wesley joined him for a beer at the bar.

"John, what happened to Thomas Callandar?"

"Jury took exactly two hours to convict him of beating his wife, almost to death. Sentenced to five years. He won't get out till 1869."

"What about his wife?"

"She served two days in jail and said she enjoyed it. Didn't have to cook, ate like a queen, slept in until 7:30 every day." They both laughed at the story. "The day she got out, we put her on a stage headed to her people in Orange County, New York. Said she was done with Thomas and his kin. Doubt we will see her again. She did want to be remembered by you. She said thank you. Said you probably saved her life. Said something about the truth setting her free. Do you understand that?

"Strangely, I do," replied Wesley

Let me ask you, Wesley, what are your plans as a Sherriff?"

"I'll take care of things down here in the southern part of the county," replied Wesley. "Hope I don't have many more cases like the Jones case, but if I do, I'm more than ready, thanks to you, John. Meanwhile, I'm going to farm and grow a family."

"Wesley, I envy you. I hope we work together again soon."

"Whoa, John! I want a little downtime here. Speaking of which, I have a wife to dance with. Enough talking, Officer Day. I have something called a honeymoon to concentrate on."

John Day laughed, slapped Wesley on the back, and proposed a toast. "Wesley, all the best to you, your bride, and your ready-made family." They clinked their beer glasses together and drained them together.

Wesley smiled and walked off to find Hope, his bride. He saw her dancing with friends, smiling and laughing.

Wesley smiled and walked over to her. "May I have this dance, Mrs. Langdon?"

"Forever, Sherriff Wesley Langdon."